DRAGON'S FLAME

RED PLANET DRAGONS OF TAJSS BOOK ELEVEN

MIRANDA MARTIN

CONTENTS

FALLON

"*T*hanks, Fallon. I don't know how I'd get everything done without everyone's help."

I smile at Kate, shaking my head as I pick up the stack of place settings. They're made of a variety of multi-colored reeds, natural stones with earth-toned striations, and Errol's delicate meteorite glass. They glimmer and shine subtly, beautiful works of art in their own right. They also feel quite sturdy, so I have a feeling they'll be borrowed for other ceremonies and events in the future.

It's a nice feeling, knowing we're likely creating traditions that future generations will follow. There was just so much sameness, first on the ship, and then in those tunnels we found ourselves in. It never really felt like we were carving any kind of a path, to be honest.

"I'm happy to help," I say sincerely. "And let me know if you need anything else," I add, adjusting my hold on my pretty burden. "I mean it."

And I do.

With all Kate has done for me and the other women from our group, helping out with her mating ceremony feels like so little to give back. To her and Errol. I really don't think we could ever repay him fully for saving us while we were stranded in the desert, let alone for reuniting us with the rest of the people from our ship.

Kate and Errol are the reason for this new life we have, this life that actually has room for more than survival. A life that's so much better than anything I could have dreamed of just weeks before in those tunnels.

Kate's smile grows at my response, her face glowing with happiness. She's definitely head over heels for Errol, and it shows in the best way possible.

"I'll definitely take you up on that offer," she murmurs. "But you might regret giving me that blanket go-ahead," she warns.

I grin back, shaking my head as I turn to go. "I know I won't," I say confidently.

She laughs as I leave the corner of Errol's workroom that she's commandeered for ceremony preparations. Though, honestly, much of the cave system has been taken over with the preparations, from the main cave where we have our communal gatherings and dinners, to the individual caves along the valley walls and the other natural corridors and offshoots leading out.

Life is hard here on Tajss, even in this new and better version of it.

I'm fully on board with seizing any opportunity to add some fun and good feelings where we can. And the others feel the same way, which is why the prep is taking over a lot of our space with no one complaining about it. Everyone is so excited at the prospect of the celebration that we're happily going all out.

Though maybe everyone isn't exactly completely accu-rate. Not when I consider those in the city. Many of the Zmaj there aren't so gung-ho about the celebration, about any return to what they call the "old ways."

As far as I can tell, their reservations aren't so much about the mating ceremony itself, but about the other traditions that fell by the wayside after the inter-planetary wars that led to The Devastation here on Tajss. An end to the technologically advanced, thriving society that once existed here before the war that ended it all.

When our small scouting group first crash-landed on Tajss, the only inkling we had that there might be more on this planet—or at least that there might have been more at some point—were the tunnels that Gomul was kind enough to allow us to live in after he rescued us from the monsters that attacked us while we were out in the open desert.

Easy prey.

Gomul—another Zmaj that we owe our lives to.

Those underground tunnels we lived in for years were clearly created and not natural, with well-engineered supports to prevent cave-ins, and a clearly ordered plan to the straight, wide corridors.

Tunnels like that indicated some kind of society, some kind of technology to dig so much so precisely, and to know how to ensure it was safe and supported. Those tunnels were actually the perfect place for us to stay, protected from the sun and patrolled by Gomul. However, as practical and safe as those tunnels were, they'd become almost unlivable.

All because of Annabel.

As important as physical needs like food and shelter are, they aren't everything. We found that out the hard way. As time passed, it became clear that Annabel wasn't fit to lead, but nobody knew what to do about it. Her grip on all of us was stifling. Petty, lazy, and dictatorial, she'd gotten worse every day, the power plainly going to her head.

I don't know what damaged her, what made her the way

she was. She was definitely on the fast track to her brain imploding—and still is, most likely, which really is a shame. There was a time when I respected her forthrightness, her push forward and take no prisoners attitude that got things done, cut through bullshit. That time is long ago now. It's buried under the resentment and disgust I feel towards her. I couldn't be happier to have left her "guidance."

We lived in fear of angering her and having to deal with retribution. She'd become the dictator of our small group. Nobody can truly thrive in such a toxic environment.

So, yes. I am glad that Kate had the guts to take a stand against Annabel, to leave what we thought was the only safe place on this planet. She took a chance for a better life and gave us an avenue to hope. It paid off in a way I could never have predicted. I never thought there could be more survivors from our ship, or that they'd be working with the Zmaj native to Tajss.

But that was what we found. A possible future.

I liked the city we first saw, the marvel of engineering left over from the height of Zmaj civilization.

I like the community here in the small cave system even more. The smaller group feels like a real family, one that wasn't even present on the ship, if I'm honest. There were too many people and too much regulation to foster a real sense of community there, every day too scheduled, our lives too clinical.

This place...I feel like a part of something real. Something that isn't held together with rules and regulations or a clear hierarchy, but rather with personal relationships and a sense of cooperation.

We're all in this together.

Despite my hard-won defenses, the prickly exterior that developed over the course of my less-than-perfect child-hood, I feel like I'm part of a whole. A gentle feeling that I never thought I would feel, not with how I was raised, anyway. My father was more an impersonal ship commander than any kind of parent to me. I learned to divorce my feelings early on. Well, all the softer feelings. Anger held on just fine, thank you very much. It's a good fuel when you need it. And I needed it.

I push thoughts of him away. I hated him, but he's gone now. And just to put some messed-up icing on that cake, I now feel a twisted sense of guilt about the hard feelings I had towards him while he was alive.

Life. Isn't it grand?

I shake my head at myself. Negativity isn't really all that productive, though I can find myself sinking into it if I'm not careful. It's like a pair of comfortable, old shoes. Fits like a glove.

But the reality is, I feel like I belong somewhere now, and I don't need those defenses as much. I have people to turn to, people who care about me, not just as someone who is necessary in a practical sense, but on a personal level.

That feels...good. Really good. I've never felt as close to anyone as I do to the women here.

And sure, some of the dragons are just as boneheaded as human men can be, like my dearly departed father, but...not quite in the same way. Their arrogance and domineering personalities seem more rooted in their prowess as warriors, in the traditions they've held on to.

Mating ceremonies not included, apparently. Not for all of them.

I look up at a sudden round of cheers, and I slow my walk to take in the scene in the flat, open space next to me.

The Zmaj of the Tribe have been participating in various warrior contests of skills, from hand-to-hand combat, to footraces, distance jumping (even more impressive than it sounds because they can use their wings to propel them forward farther than human men could), accuracy with a lochaber (a massive staff-like weapon held in two hands with a sharp blade at the end) that involves moving targets, and a few more events that I've seen but don't fully comprehend.

The scene before me now is another bout of hand-to-hand combat. Bashir stands over Melchior, who is flat on his back—and clearly unhappy about it.

I falter a little as I walk by, feeling the celebratory mood of the games start to turn. They're supposed to be a fun time, something for the competitive bunch to do to add to the festivities leading up to the mating ceremony itself. However, I can see as well as feel the shift in the mood as Melchior slowly gets to his feet.

Maybe they would have been better off with a nice, safe test of skill.

Like a chess tournament.

Melchior's snarl and the clenched fists at his sides show that he's fighting the bijass, that primal part of the Zmaj that wants to dominate. The part of them that is almost pure animal instinct.

"One, I am myself," Arawn says clearly into the tense silence, his voice firm.

A ripple of reaction shudders through Melchior, halting the slow progress he was making towards Bashir.

"Two...together we are stronger," Bashir continues, his eyes locked with the opponent he has already beaten, his voice clear and strong.

Melchior takes a deep breath, rolling his shoulders.

"Three," he starts hoarsely, his fists slowly loosening. "Three, survival of the group matters."

The tension immediately drops.

I breathe out a sigh of relief along with everyone else watching.

When I first heard of the Edicts, the Creed of the Tribe,

an echo of their core values, I didn't truly understand how important they were for the very survival of the Tribe. But after living with them for a longer period of time, I now understand all too well. This isn't the first time I've seen the mantra help control the bijass, and I'm sure it won't be the last either.

And still, despite displays like this, and many of their often domineering and arrogant personalities, none of that has prevented the numerous human-dragon matings.

Even as I have that thought, Penelope hurries over to Bashir, who smiles at her, the interruption fully breaking the last bit of lingering tension. She says something to him that has him chuckling and shaking his head as she grins back.

The couplings seem to work—both the dragon men and the women are thriving as partners.

I can appreciate that, appreciate that people are happy. Even if I don't ever see myself mating or in any romantic relationship of my own, for that matter. It just isn't for me. I like the other women, but apart from that, I prefer to keep to myself. Make my own decisions without worrying what someone else will think.

Even though I'm not looking for any kind of partner, I'm still glad we followed Kate here. Maybe the others will be happier in a relationship like that. To each their own.

I'm so deep in my thoughts on the matter that I don't even notice there's a large, dragon-man-shaped obstruction in my path until I'm nearly on top of him.

I yelp as I quickly take a step back, rebalancing the stack of mats in my arms and glare up at Arawn.

He looks way too pleased with himself, as usual. He's obviously put himself in my path on purpose. The standard ridiculous seven feet tall and lithely muscled for a dragon, he's impressively cut for his main role as the tribe's leatherworker.

7

He's not terrible to look at, with a masculine face set off with neat horns, bright orange-red scales, and striking aqua-green eyes that contrast nicely with the warmth of his scales. Added to the leathery wings and the sinuous tail, he really is a sight. He's also quick and clever. Intelligent.

Too bad he's so overly impressed with himself. And expects everyone else to feel the same way about him.

"Excuse me," I mutter, stepping to the side to go around him, but he just matches my step. Blocking my path. Again. Grunting, I step to the other side. But he matches me again.

I'm just getting irritated now. You know what? Fine. Rather than trying to go around, I change strategy and march straight at him next.

He's clearly not expecting it. Eyes widening, he steps back automatically before he catches himself and stops yet again.

I scowl, really annoyed now. I do not have the patience for this. I look back up at him, meeting his mischievous eyes.

"Arawn, I am not in the mood," I bite out. I lift up my burden and give it a little shake. "I need to get these to the others."

The glimmer in his eyes softens and he nods slightly. He finally catches the drift. Though it took actual words to get through his thick skull.

"My apologies," he murmurs, stepping to the side, this time out of my path. He gestures to the open way. "Please."

I incline my head, moving past him, now that I have a chance. Before he changes his mind and decides to mess with me some more. As I walk away, I can feel that tingle along my back that lets me know he's still watching me. I suppress the shiver of awareness, annoyed at myself now at my response to his attention.

I breathe a silent sigh of relief as I turn the corner and the line of sight is broken, my shoulders dropping. Shaking off my irritation—and that uncomfortable awareness—I deliver the mats and go on with the rest of the tasks I have to get done.

We all have to work together here, or we won't survive. It's as simple and as serious as that. I don't mind. I like feeling productive.

By the time it's time for the pre-ceremonial communal meal, I'm ready for a break.

The food laid out across the large table looks delicious, and I'm happy to see there's a large bowl filled with Delilah's special sauce. It's just as much of a hit here as it was on the ship.

"Man, I'm so glad you figured out how to recreate this," I murmur appreciatively as I ladle some onto the meat and vegetables I already have on my plate. "It makes anything and everything taste amazing."

Delilah chuckles as she refills the bowl from the pot she made the sauce in.

"I'm glad everyone enjoys it. It's a good recipe to have in my pocket for bribes," she adds with a wink that makes me chuckle.

"Very true," I agree.

The first time we had a communal meal here, I was blown away by the spread. Not only was there meat, there were also vegetables and fruits. Along with the herbs and other spices for flavoring. The food was simple, but varied and good. Even without the introduction of epis to our small group, I really think we would have been healthier overall just from the better diet.

Though, admittedly, not nearly as healthy as we are now that we have that plant in our lives. The difference is night and day between before and after taking it. I actually feel like day-to-day life is no longer a struggle. Before the epis, I would always be soaked in sweat no matter my physical activity level, constantly fighting weakness.

Now that we're on a dose of it, I've put on weight, along with Kate and Nora. And it looks good on us! I like seeing them healthier. I'm sure Lanie, Ashlee, and Addison have put some on in the city as well. They seem just as happy there as we are here.

Plate now full, I wander around to chat with everyone gathered. The communal meals are a good time to decompress from the day, let go of worries. While I'm moving, I feel that familiar tingle, that sense of being watched, even though I'm distracted by the conversation around me. I move my head casually, scanning out of the corner of my eye.

There.

Arawn is sitting next to a few other Zmaj, but his eyes are focused on me rather than his companions. Why is he always watching me? And why is it so damn distracting every time?

"Fallon."

I turn at Errol's voice, smiling at him as I step closer.

"Yes?"

"I was wondering if you could give me an opinion on the design of this cloth..."

I listen, giving my two cents as he describes the design, all the while conscious of the fact that Arawn is still watching me. My eyes are inexorably drawn to him once more, but when I accidentally make eye contact, I quickly look away again.

Focus!

Trying to shut out my fascination with the Zmaj craftsman, I attempt to focus on the conversation. I don't want Errol to think I'm an idiot. I'm no fashion designer, but I give him my opinion, figuring it will balance out with everyone else's. It's honestly really adorable how completely into this ceremony he is, how he wants every detail to be perfect, from the place mats, to the clothes, to the decorations.

It shows how much he cares. It's really refreshing how the

Zmaj men don't hide how deeply they feel for their women. As long as it isn't directed at me anyway.

Our conversation is already winding down when Bashir calls out to Errol, taking his attention.

"Excuse me," he says politely.

I nod, stepping back, almost bumping into Nora. "Oops, sorry," I say, changing direction.

She smiles. "No problem," she says in that quiet voice. "Hey, would you like to play a game of chess with me? There's a board free over there."

I turn at her gesture, my eyes seeking Arawn out automatically as I do. Damn it. What is this draw he has for me?

I force myself to turn away, happy that at least his attention had been diverted so he didn't notice me looking at him.

"Sure, let's play," I agree, determined to distract my betraying eyes.

Errol, Ormarr, and some of the others worked together to create actual boards and pieces for checkers and chess, fully taken by the games that we humans introduced to them. Not surprising considering the competitive drive they all seem to naturally have.

As if on cue, Arawn growls, deep in a game next to us. Rolling my eyes at the sound, I sit down across from Nora, taking another bite of my food.

She grabs one of the pawns and holds it behind her back. "Black or white?" she asks.

Hmm. "White."

She opens her fist, revealing a black pawn.

"Damn," I say good-naturedly. "Guess you're white."

She smiles. "You always pick white."

"I do?" I ask, surprised at that. "Good to know."

We set up the board quickly, and Nora makes her first move. The first time we sat down and she beat me, I have to admit I was surprised. I've been giving her a run for her money every time since. It's usually a toss-up over who will win any game between us—we're so well matched. So the game should capture all of my attention. Emphasis on should. Unfortunately, even the rousing game of strategy isn't enough to capture the entirety of my focus.

I find my eye wandering over to Arawn multiple times.

"He just stopped looking at you."

I quickly turn my eyes back to the game. "What?"

"Arawn," Nora says, a slight smile tugging at the corners of her mouth. "He just stopped staring at you." She looks in his direction. "Update—he's looking at you again."

I feel that tingle that would have let me know that even if Nora hadn't.

"He's probably watching our game," I mutter, the reasoning sounding lame even to my own ears.

Nora chuckles as she makes another move, taking my knight. I frown at the board.

"Well, him watching the game seems to be distracting you. Maybe I should make sure he's always around when we play," she teases.

I shake my head.

Beneath that quiet exterior lies a sharp mind that sees a lot more than people think.

"Just play," I order, making the best move I can on the current board. Nora's right. I have been letting Arawn distract me from the game, and it's showing.

The worst of it is, I'm not just looking at him to see if he's watching me.

2

ARAWN

"The return of the old ways is not wise. No matter how enamored Errol is with the idea of a water ceremony," Ladon mutters, frowning slightly.

"It is true. I do not understand how he does not worry about the troubles this could bring for us," Shidan agrees, keeping his voice just as low.

"Yes. I do not understand this desire to force us back to the old ways. Can we not simply be content with this new way of life we have been given? Is it not enough?" Astarot adds, shaking his head. "It feels very shortsighted."

My jaw clenches as I hear the group of Zmaj from the city discussing the upcoming mating ceremony as though it is a harbinger of doom. It's perfectly ridiculous. They act as though gods will descend from the sky and smite Tajss for the terrible evil of having a mating ceremony. The thought is laughable.

Though I have been consciously holding my tongue on the matter, not wanting to stir up even more trouble among this group that cannot simply accept what is happening. If anything, the traditions will return a sense of wholeness to us. I, for one, am quite glad Errol and Kate will be mating ceremonially. In my estimation, the problem is not truly with the mating ceremony, or even a real fear of returning to the old ways.

The issue really lies within many of my Zmaj brothers. I know some of them are haunted with memories of the past, fragments and nightmares that they try their best to bury where they may not affect them. It sounds like an exhausting endeavor.

I realize how fortunate I am not to be haunted by my past, not to have the same desire to pretend reality away as they seem to. I want to stay firmly here, past included.

I try not to shake my head as I listen to them continue on the same topic, discussing the upcoming water ceremony as though it denotes the end of civilization itself. I do not want to offend them or cause more tension before the ceremony, but eventually, I cannot simply allow this type of talk without at least attempting to intervene. It does not make any sense.

"You are all behaving as though the water ceremony will throw our new society into chaos," I cut in, not bothering to lower my voice as they did. I am not worried about others hearing my opinion.

My interruption is a surprise.

Perhaps they did not realize I was listening to their low conversation so intently.

It has them all glancing at each other and I can see they are trying to decide how to respond without being rude.

They are in our home now after all.

"It is everything that will come along with the ceremony," Astarot explains carefully. "Things we would not like to dredge up, now that we have moved on from them."

"The past is not all good," Ladon adds.

I sigh Now that I have inserted myself, I need to say my piece.

"Why must you look for trouble where there is none? We are speaking simply of the water ceremony, a celebration that has already brought all of us closer together. When else would all of you and your mates and children have come to our cave system?" That point has them nodding reluctantly. "And there is no rule that says we must reintroduce everything from before if we take even a sliver back. We can do as we please."

"It is not so simple," Ladon counters. "This will stir up more than just the ceremony."

"I think you are complicating the issue unnecessarily." I look around at the assembled males. "The Zmaj bloodline will continue through Kate and Errol's union, just as it has with the other matings, ensuring our survival as a people. Why shouldn't that be recognized by our ancestors in formal ceremony? It seems only fitting to me, and I do not understand this level of opposition to it."

A beat of silence where I can see them digesting this point.

"Perhaps Arawn is correct," Shidan murmurs, glancing at the others before meeting my eyes once more. "I apologize for any negativity our comments may have brought today," he adds.

I nod my head as the others murmur a similar sentiment.

I know I have not fully convinced them of my viewpoint.

I know they are choosing not to argue more in order to be polite.

But I still appreciate that they are sensitive to the fact that the ceremony is happening, and that the Tribe has no issue with it.

Nonetheless, when Illadon runs by, his short, strong little legs propelling him forward with more speed than I would have guessed, I feel a wash of relief at the distraction.

And what an adorable distraction he is. At about three years, his bright blue, green, and yellow scales attract attention, matching his yellow-green eyes. His grin is wide and happy, drawing a smile from me and the others watching.

"Illadon!" Callista calls out in a harried voice. "What did I say about behavior during the ceremony?"

I chuckle as I notice little Illadon continue to run, looking back for his small shadow.

He is obviously attempting to show off for Ragnar and Olivia's adorable red-haired daughter, Zoe.

Her much more subtle scales glimmer as they catch the light, her short little horns and round cheeks just as cute.

I can certainly appreciate his desire to impress a female. It is embarrassing to realize he seems to be having more success than I am currently.

Judging by Zoe's gurgling laughter as she runs after him as fast as she can, her bright blue eyes sparkling, it is working quite well actually.

Ladon shakes his head as only a long-suffering parent can, but a grin tugs at the corners of his mouth as well. He is obviously quite proud of his son, which is a wonderful sight to see.

"Illadon is into everything now, his sense of adventure sometimes a little too strong for his mother," he explains. "Sometimes I fear he will drive her to tie him up in an attempt to keep him away from trouble." When the child veers to the right, aiming for the flame of a candle, Ladon moves quickly, stepping forward and scooping the little troublemaker into his arms, the child shrieking with laughter.

"Oh, man. I can't wait for when this baby is here, but I'm also a little scared at the same time," Lana remarks as she walks over, her eyes on Illadon, hand on her small round belly. "That looks like a lot of work."

The curvy, dark-haired female is even curvier now, her body just beginning to visibly change with her own child.

"Do not worry," Astarot reassures her, wrapping an arm around her and leaning down to kiss her temple, the love in his eyes clear, the hand he places over her stomach, over their child, protective. "I will run after our little one, so you will not have to."

She chuckles, shaking her head as she turns to kiss his cheek.

"I'll hold you to that," she warns, smiling.

"That's what I tell Drosdan when he makes me promises." Sarah is approaching, Drosdan by her side. She is further along in her pregnancy, her middle rounder and larger. Her mate watches her attentively.

"I mean every one of those promises," Drosdan reassures her. "And any more you would like me to make as well."

Sarah shakes her head, patting his cheek.

"It's difficult to be mad at him for being the reason I'm in this condition when he's being so sweet," she chuckles.

"I know exactly what you mean," Lana agrees, looking up at her own mate with affection.

When Penelope and Bashir also wander over, hand in hand, I move back somewhat. Everyone has their mate, and some have a child or a child on the way. It makes me ache for the same. It is too much, on the heels of the conversation of the ceremony.

"Excuse me," I murmur.

Determined to keep my own spirits high, where they usually are, I step away from the heartwarming tableau and move to the kitchen, somewhere I do not have to be so careful.

Delilah looks up as I near, a smile wreathing her pretty face, bright and white against her warm brown skin.

"Arawn—tell me you're here to help."

The kitchen is busy indeed, multiple people chopping, washing dishes, hauling in ingredients, discarding refuse. The preparations for the meal we will have at the ceremony are fully underway. I smile back.

"I am here to help."

"Perfect! I need some help breaking down this meat over here."

I follow her over to the large slab waiting to be cut up.

"What size do you require?" I ask, picking up the meat cleaver.

"Small chunks. About this big, please," she adds, holding up her fingers to show me the size.

"Easy enough."

She slaps me on the back. "I knew I could count on you," she announces, already spinning to go back to the actual cooking.

I get to work, much happier performing this task than listening to others complain about something they obviously cannot change.

As I do, I watch Delilah move confidently through the kitchen, directing others. There was a time when I thought perhaps Delilah and I might mate. She is quite attractive, intelligent, and her cooking skills are universally admired—with good reason.

But she never gave me any indication she wanted me in that way, and our relationship has since developed into a comfortable rapport that is more like a brother and sister than anything romantic. We bicker, play with each other, but nothing more than that. She is a good friend, one I know I can count on, but I also know now we will never be more than that. I have accepted it without much, if any, difficulty.

Now, Fallon, on the other hand...

Her gorgeous face flashes in my mind. Fine boned, with a delicate jaw, slightly upturned bright blue eyes, and a generous, wide mouth, she draws me like no other. I want to touch that soft skin, run my fingers through her honey-blond hair, skim them over those delicious curves. I suppress a growl at the thought, feeling my body stir even now. It is the same whenever my mind turns to her.

Unfortunately, she seems completely resistant to the obvious magnetism between us. Determinedly so. I know she watches me, just as I watch her. But she does not act on the attraction. It is frustrating, but I refuse to concede. Not with Fallon.

I cannot simply fall into a sibling relationship with her as I have with Delilah. It would be impossible. So I continue to try.

As I've watched her from afar, I've learned more about her, and her own frustrations. Her caged heart rails against the reality that she is too soft to hunt and fend for herself here on Tajss. My own heart, sensing that, has begun to beat in unison with hers.

I feel a pull that is deeper than mere surface attraction—though she is nothing less than a true piece of art, one that lives and breathes. My initial attraction to Delilah pales in comparison to what I feel for Fallon. Truthfully, they are not even comparable. Fallon is a true treasure. My treasure.

The yearning for her is stronger than anything I have ever experienced before, the urge to have her, to protect her, to keep her safe is overwhelming. Undeniable.

I finish my tasks in the kitchen with a focused intensity,

hoping to steal a few moments with the object of my desire before everyone else arrives. To that end, I arrive early for the pre-ceremony in one of the lower caverns. But Fallon is nowhere to be found.

Where could she be? I thought I would find all of Kate's inner circle aiding in preparations. I do see Nora. Perhaps she will know. The quiet woman looks up as I approach, her gaze questioning.

"Do you know where I could find Fallon?" I ask politely, not wanting to appear too intense. Nora is one of the more fragile of the human females, soft-spoken and shy.

"Oh, she must already be with Kate. I'm heading over there right now to help put the finishing touches on the cere-monial cloak she will wear."

Ah, yes. I have heard of the cloak, from Errol and from others. He fashioned jewels from the collected meteorite glass and the women of the village have been working dili-gently to adorn the cloak with them.

We males are also under strict orders not to try to see Kate until just before the recital of the vows Errol and she will exchange. It is an odd aspect of their human ceremonial tradi-tions, but I do not mind their outright refusal of any of us seeing her before the ceremony. They have adjusted to a great deal here on Tajss. This is a simple enough request. But I do feel a sharp disappointment at not being able to see Fallon as I had hoped.

"Thank you, Nora," I murmur, taking a step back.

She nods, hurrying away to continue with her duties.

With nothing else to occupy my time now, I join those still working, lending a hand where I can.

If nothing else, the naysayers cannot deny that the cere-mony has brought us all closer together, the effort made towards a common goal helping cement our bonds even further.

Eventually, all the work is done, and we all sit down to anticipate the ceremony.

The ceremonial decor looks beautiful, all of our efforts resulting in a wonderful setting for the vows to be exchanged. Reeds and large, pale blossoms adorn the area and the raised platform. I personally worked on that platform, paneling the sturdy piece carefully so it will last.

This is our first mating ceremony, but I doubt it will be the last now that Errol has demanded one. It only makes sense to build features that will last, that can be used multiple times both for mating ceremonies and any others we might like to have in the future.

I worked with Bashir and several others to incorporate meteorite glass into the design of the platform as well, and now that everything is displayed together, I can truly appreciate the brilliant shine of the adornment.

It calls the eye, sparkling and glimmering in the light of the many candles placed around it, casting a soft light over all those gathered, along with the sunlight streaming down.

It is a poor rival indeed for Fallon's beauty when she finally joins the other females. My heart races at the sight, drinking her in, lingering on her hair, almost as yellow as the sands near the most treacherous areas on Tajss, where no one lives anymore after the mass migration of the dangerous beasts. A unique color—and fitting for her. It is pulled back at the sides of her head, swept back to leave her beautiful face bare, the strands tumbling down her back in a smooth waterfall my hands itch to touch.

Her eyes scan the area before they lock with my own, a mysterious cast to the blue in this lighting. In the spirit of the moment, she awards me a smile that warms me. But she does not allow her attention to linger, her gaze continuing on around. My heart sinks a bit as she looks away. I do not know why she refuses to acknowledge this between us. However, I do not have time to dwell on the topic.

The murmur of conversation continues around me, the anticipation for the ceremony building. Luckily, we do not have to wait long. My attention is thankfully taken by the coming declaration of abiding love about to unfold in front of the gathered group.

I join the other males of the Tribe, all of us dressed in traditional robes with our lochabers in hand. We arrange ourselves in two lines facing each other, creating a corridor for those participating in the ceremony to walk through.

Errol and his father Gomul are the first to pass, Errol's arm around Gomul's shoulders, the two radiating happiness as they pass between us.

Errol's traditional robe is adorned with pieces of meteorite glass, the shimmering pieces drawing the eye to him, though the joy beaming from his face would have done the same.

We hum in unison to mark their entry, the low vibrato of our voices blending together, symbolizing we are one.

Gomul takes the place of respect next to Commander Visidion who will be performing the ceremony, stepping onto the platform.

Errol takes his place, leaving room for his mate next to him. As soon as he is in place, all of us turn to look for Kate.

Her appearance does not disappoint. She steps out of the cave where she has been preparing, her dress sparkling brightly in the sun with small bits of the same glass her mate wears.

Kate is truly resplendent in the silvery gown and long cloak trailing behind her, the meteorite glass catching the light and reflecting softly. Her fiery hair is caught in an intricate style at the top of her head, subtle color applied to her pale, pretty face.

She is a dazzling sight, the shimmer of her dress matching the radiance of her face, her joy at the coming ceremony as profound as her mate's.

Errol cannot take his eyes off of her.

She stands at the top of the ramp for a moment as the other females pick up the train of her dress and help her walk down towards us. One of them is Fallon. She may not shimmer as much as Kate, but she draws my eye nonetheless.

At the signal, we raise our lochabers, extending our arms up so the blades cross at the top of the space between the lines we have formed, creating a tunnel for Kate to walk through. As she does so, her eyes are locked on Errol and only Errol. My heart aches at the sight, imaging Fallon looking at me in that same manner.

Even as I think it, Fallon's eyes meet mine as she walks past with Kate's train in hand. The eye contact is searing.

But she looks away after only a beat, her cheeks flushing slightly.

Patience.

The females let go of Kate's dress, spreading the train out in a pretty fan as Errol takes her hands and guides her so they are facing each other in front of Visidion.

Everyone's eyes are on Errol and Kate as the Commander lays his hands on theirs.

Except mine.

They continue to stray to Fallon. And find her own on mine more than once. I shift restlessly.

"Errol. Your heart has yearned and has been answered. Is this the female you would share water with?"

It is.

My inner thought is echoed by Errol's voice as I imagine Fallon and myself in front of Visidion, exchanging the traditional vows, committing to each other. That is all I can think of as the ceremony continues.

Drosdan and Padraig walk forward, carrying a large barrel of water between them that they set down in front of the couple.

The ceremony continues, Visidion ceding his place to Gomul, who steps in easily, well versed in this ceremony he performed many times in the past.

"Water brings life. In sharing water, you commit one to another, and both to all of us. Our future rests on you."

He pours water over both Errol's and Kate's heads.

Before they then do the same to each other.

"I give you my water," Errol says clearly as he pours it over Kate's head.

"I take your water," she answers.

Fallon looks over at me at those words.

But then looks away quickly again when our eyes meet.

This is a kind of torture that I could not have imagined. I am so distracted that I do not even realize when the ceremony ends. Only the cheers of those around me draw my attention back. I add my own raucous roar of approval to the sound as Errol swings his mate into his arms and kisses her deeply, clearly uncaring of who sees.

This is a human tradition we all approve of without question. My eyes go to Fallon, where they always desire to be when in her vicinity. Delilah told me of their tradition of kissing the female after the ceremony. And all I could think of then and now are Fallon's soft lips. Yes, this is a tradition that I would be more than happy to include in any ceremony I have with my mate.

But first, the real celebration is set to begin now that the ceremony is over. When Errol sets Kate back on her feet, her eyes are sparkling, her cheeks flushed.

As if this is the silent signal, we all rush towards the newly mated couple, offering our congratulations. The mood is joyous and light, even the dissenters' grumblings quiet now as we stream into the communal area.

It too has been transformed to match the occasion. Candles have been scattered everywhere, placed strategically to avoid burning the lovely creamy blooms that pour forth from the vines Delilah and Penelope have successfully uprooted and transplanted into the soil here.

Meteorite glass twines around some of them, artfully placed with a subtle wire that also supports the candles, careful metalwork done by Errol and me specifically for the decorations. We wanted to ensure everyone's safety while also delivering the vision Errol and Kate had for the day. The final look glimmers and shimmers, creating a dreamy atmosphere that I am certain we will always remember.

It is nice to do something that is not only purely for survival. It adds a softness to life that I didn't realize I missed. The food is set out on one of the longer tables, with seats and tables arranged throughout, small areas to mingle and talk to each other.

I go to the table, talking to those around me as I fill my plate. But my attention is not on my words. My eyes find Fallon's bright head just as she tilts it back to laugh at something Kate said, her happiness beaming out of her.

I ache to be closer. But I take my plate and move to a nearby table, not wanting to intrude upon her time with her friends on this special day.

Delilah arranges people to move around the crowd, passing out cups full of the britang, the fermented drink we create from the fruit in season. This last batch was particularly good, and everyone takes the offering with a smile.

"A toast!" Fallon announces once everyone has a cup in their hand. "To the happy couple—I've never seen anyone so disgustingly happy." Chuckles ripple through the room, and she waits for them to die down. "It's a joy to be around you," she adds more seriously, the sincerity in her voice clear even from some distance. "Congratulations."

The females take a sip as she does, prompting the rest of us to do the same. The sweet taste of the britang hits my tongue, the fiery bite of it sliding down my throat and warming me.

A few others give similar congratulatory words to the mated couple, but I do not pay attention to the words. My attention is all for Fallon. But I take a deep drink every time it is appropriate. And I watch as Fallon does the same.

The mood is merry, the food plentiful, the drink flowing. Everyone wants to celebrate, make the most of this occasion. As soon as my cup is empty, someone ensures it is full.

I am weak with my longing for Fallon, so I drink. And drink. Attempt to dull that harsh edge of frustration as I watch her.

I watch as she drinks as well, laughing and talking with her friends, eating and dancing. For some, that might signal an opportunity to try once more. But not for me.

As I watch her laughing, her face flushed with drink, I feel the pang of opportunity lost. I would not dream of taking advantage or her or any other female in a drunken state.

Downing the last of my drink, I stand, taking a moment to allow the room to settle around me.

Then I make my own way over to the dancing, Zmaj and humans alike whirling and hopping to the music from the drums and flutes played by a small group of human women and some of my Zmaj brethren. I fashioned a few of the instruments myself.

The flutes are similar to the old calling whistles of Tajss, so not completely alien. The drums are made from the skins of some of the beasts we have hunted, the sound coming from them calling to me in a primitive way.

I do not fully understand this dancing that the humans

have brought to Tajss, but it seems easy enough. I know how to move my body and doing so to music is not any more difficult than following a beast and striking at the right time.

I allow the rhythm to flow through me, my attention on Fallon even as I dance with Penelope and then Delilah, copying their movements, learning how to compliment them.

"You're good!" Delilah offers, grinning as she moves with me.

I smile back, enjoying myself only partly because of the drink. When I find myself without a partner, I continue to dance by myself, the exertion of my body a different kind of release. It feels good to let go, even just this much. Perhaps I am gaining a better understanding of why the humans do this at celebrations.

Fallon

I feel the buzz of the alcohol as I dance, watching Arawn move. The ceremony has me feeling...something. Something I didn't expect. Something uncomfortable that I push away as I watch Arawn. But I don't move my gaze away from him. He moves smoothly, picking up how to dance quickly. It isn't surprising, considering how physical he is, how in tune with his own body.

I just didn't expect it would turn me on like it's doing.

Though, to be honest, he could be doing the Macarena and I'd probably still feel hot under the collar.

It's just him.

I down the rest of my drink. Liquid courage.

. . .

Arawn

A female has just twirled into me! My arms, thinking for themselves, immediately reach out to steady her. I would never have been caught so unaware had I not had so much to drink. Nor would I have ever lost track of Fallon so completely that seeing her in my arms would be a shock. But I am not so far gone that I waste the opportunity, deep in drink or not.

Fallon looks up at me, and her eyes open wide.

"Sorry," she murmurs, her hands coming up to settle on my chest. "I didn't see you there."

Despite her words, she continues to move with me, with the music, giving no indication that she wants to move away. I do not want to deny her tumbling directly into my arms.

"I do not mind," I return, moving with her before she can decide to pull away.

She moves with me, her eyes still locked with mine as her hands slide up to clasp my shoulders.

The beat of the drums seeps into my blood as Fallon moves sinuously against me, her eyes dreamy as she dances to the music.

Dancing is quickly becoming my favorite pastime. Perhaps I can convince the others to have a dance after every meal.

Her breasts brush against my chest. Her hands caress my chest, my arms. Her lips part slightly with her breath, her eyes half-lidded as she presses her hips closer. Brushing against the part of me that is now fully awake. And throbbing for more.

I grit my teeth as she turns around, pushing her backside against me, the soft curves cradling me perfectly as she raises her arms, one of her hands sliding into my hair, the other cupping the side of my neck.

A flash of heat pierces me. My jaw clenches hard and my hands squeeze down on her hips.

Too much. This is too much for me to handle.

"Excuse me," I say, gently extracting myself from her lingering hands. "I must..."

I do not know what reason to give, so I let my sentence trail off as I step back from her alluring body.

It is painful. I do not want to do it, but I also know I need to. I do not have full control over myself. I do not trust myself.

I make my way through the revelers, keeping my focus on the path before me, and not on the beautiful female I just left behind. Not on the throbbing of my cock, demanding more.

I stifle a snarl as I exit the cavern and walk swiftly for my own cave, needing to be alone. I need to relieve myself, relieve some of this pressure that feels as though it might kill me.

I do not realize I am being followed until I step into my cave and someone else steps in directly after me.

"I am never going to drink so much britang again," I mutter under my breath as I turn to see who it is.

I blink at Fallon, my irritated words leaving me immediately.

Why is she..."

"Fallon?" I ask, confused. "What—?"

Before I can finish my question, she is closing the distance between us, her hands sliding up my chest again.

But there are no drums here. No music. No other people to dilute the gesture. To make it mean anything else.

"Fallon..."

"Arawn," she murmurs, pushing me back.

I move, my hands going down to rest on her hips as she

slowly crowds me back, until the backs of my legs hit the bed. She tumbles me back onto it, coming down on top of me.

Is this a dream?

"Fallon, I do not think—"

This time my words are cut off not by her words, but by the touch of her soft lips to mine. Caressing. Coaxing. Asking to be let in.

I groan, my hands sliding up her delicate back as I return her kiss, my tongue sliding against hers, the tart taste of her mouth exactly what I want.

I am only a male. There is only so much I can deny her.

She hums in the back of her throat as she deepens the kiss even more, shimmying so her legs are on either side of my hips as she attacks my mouth.

I am a more than willing recipient of what she has to give. I touch her everywhere, everywhere that I have been dreaming of. I run my hands through that silky hair, slide my hands down to cup the curves of her backside, knead the curve of her waist.

I want all of her.

Her curious fingers slide down the skin of my chest, across my arms, taking the robe with them. Down my taut stomach, to the fastening of my waistband. The ceremonial robe is the only piece of clothing I am wearing. With a firm tug, she undoes it, sliding it down and off my body.

Sitting up astride me, her eyes scan my length hungrily. They stop on my cock, lying thick and hard and ready across my stomach.

Breathing hard, she swallows as she reaches out to take hold of me.

I grit my teeth as her soft, small hand wraps around my thickness, the pleasure excruciating. I allow her one stroke, her curious thumb rubbing along the ridges that line the length.

Two.

That is all I can take without embarrassing myself. I flip us easily, her surprised yelp making me smile as she lands softly on her back underneath me.

I meet her eyes as I reach for her clothing, watching for any sign that she does not want to continue. But she only bites her lip and helps me divest her of the pretty dress she made for the occasion, her eyes heated as she watches me watch her.

I swallow as I take in her beauty, completely bared to me for the first time. Her body is so soft, so delicate. The curves of her breasts, the indent of her long waist, the softness of her hip. And the glowing, silky skin.

"I must taste," I growl, bending down to the pale pink tip of one breast.

She sighs as I take the firm tip into my mouth, her hands sliding into my hair.

I lick at her, suck at her as my other hand kneads the softness of her other breast, wanting to touch and taste her everywhere at once.

I let go of the firm little nub, lick my way over to the other and give it a hard suck that has Fallon writhing under me.

After rubbing my face against the soft undersides, I kiss my way down her smooth belly.

Down to the softest, pinkest part of her.

I push her thighs apart, ever so gently, and then I bury my face against her, licking along the wet valley. She cries out, her hands gripping my scalp as I flick my tongue against her. Growling, I bend her legs at the knee and spear her with my tongue, the taste of her more addictive than any drink.

Her scream is hoarse this time as she bucks against me, as I drink down her pleasure and want only more.

Rising up, I take the base of my cock in my hand and rub the leaking head up and down her cleft, watching her face as I do. Her eyes open, her hair sticking to the damp skin of her face now, her chest flushed.

I stop my up-and-down motions and pause at her entrance.

"Beautiful Fallon. I want to be inside you," I whisper, my own voice hoarse and low. My need clear. Not that I want to hide it from her.

"Yes," she whispers, spreading her legs farther apart.

I shudder at the acceptance.

Slow.

She is small.

With that thought in mind, I carefully push into her, her body slowly allowing mine in.

She makes small sounds in the back of her throat as I hold her firmly in place for my thrusts, each one bringing me closer and closer to being fully seated. When my hips finally meet hers, sweat drips down my face with the effort the slow pace takes. But her pleasure is more important than my own. I want her to enjoy this first time between us.

Reaching between us, I use my thumb to rub at the firm little nub that gives her so much pleasure. She immediately softens underneath me, her hips thrusting up against me. When I look up at her face once more, her eyes are closed, a slight frown between her brows.

Experimentally, I pull out and thrust back in, the ridged spine along my cock rubbing against that sensitive nub.

She cries out, her eyes opening slightly.

"More, Arawn," she demands.

I shudder at the words. I can give her more. Taking a deep breath, I build up a slow rhythm, still conscious of the fact that she is so much smaller than me. So much more breakable.

But when she starts to meet me thrust for thrust, her hips pushing up against mine, I let go some of my control. Leaning over her, I brace my forearms on either side of her head. After bending down to kiss her, I allow my next thrust to be harder, I grind against her a little more.

Her hands come up to grip me, her nails digging into my back as she sings out her pleasure.

So I do it again.

And again.

Until she breaks the kiss and her neck arches, her eyes unseeing as her climax explodes through her.

I have no defense against the clenching around my own member.

I groan as my seed leaves me, my pleasure a hot, hard, all-encompassing feeling as I continue to thrust, the movement not at all controlled now.

I take in a deep breath as I let my forehead drop down on to Fallon's, feeling my arms tremble in reaction. I feel as though I have felled a great beast, one I would gladly take on again.

Fallon's hands smooth down my back soothingly as she kisses my neck. And then, between one breath and the next, she is asleep.

I chuckle to myself, caressing her cheek tenderly as I carefully pull out of her warmth and roll to the side so as not to crush her under my much larger body.

I gather her to me, feeling how ready my second cock is, but that discomfort is of no matter to me. Not with Fallon in my arms. I smooth the hair back from her face as I watch her sleep, her face so relaxed from our lovemaking.

I sigh. Her actions, drink or no, solidify what I knew we'd

both been feeling. There is no question now we have something, something undeniable.

But this is not how I imagined the first time we would come together. No commitment, both of us with cloudy heads...

I fear she will regret yielding to the call of her body and spirit come morning.

I hold her even closer, hugging the comforting warmth of her to me, but worry keeps me up well into the night.

3

FALLON

*O*h, man.

    I turn my head to the side, the piercing hammers inside my skull letting me know I may have overindulged.

Just a smidge.

Ugh.

I rub at my gritty eyes, wishing someone would just knock me out and put me out of my misery. It really doesn't help knowing I did this to myself.

All right. Game plan. I need water and I need to pee. Neither can be accomplished while I lie here. Damn it.

I take a deep breath and hold it as I force myself to sit up while my body insists it is no longer made to perform that motion. I wince as the pounding in my head sharpens, before settling down once more. I haven't had a hangover like this in who knows how long, and I would be just fine not having another one ever, thanks very much.

I carefully open my eyes, worrying it'll make the pain worse. But the sun has only barely risen, judging by the soft light coming in.

Wait.

I frown, looking around the unfamiliar cave. Where the hell...?

A sense of rising dread hits me. If this isn't my cave...

Swallowing thickly, I slowly turn to look down at the bed. Oh. Shit.

Arawn is fast asleep, his tanned, well-muscled form taking up more than half of the pallet.

I stare at him, my mouth falling open.

Stars!

What have I done? Damn it, Fallon! Exactly how much did I have to drink that this sounded like a good idea to me?

A flash of memory hits me. Of me pushing Arawn down on the bed. Oh no. Oh no no no. I slap my hands over my face, shaking my head as I feel blood rush to my cheeks.

All right, okay. I need to get a hold of myself right now and get the heck out of here ASAP unless I want an awkward morning-after chat with Arawn.

In bed.

With both of us stark naked.

Yeah, no.

I gingerly take my hands off my face and study the bed. The blankets are woven around his legs and mine, entwining us together. I carefully extricate myself from the blankets, making sure not to move the bed too much or to jostle his sleeping form. I don't particularly want to talk to him about this. Ever.

I mentally slap myself. This has got to be one of the crowning achievements of my life when it comes to sheer stupidity. Ranking right up there with staying with Annabel as long as we did.

I freeze as Arawn shifts in the bed, a slight frown appearing on his previously sleep-slack face.

I hold my breath, but he relaxes again and sinks back into a deep sleep.

Letting out a silent sigh of relief, I draw my legs out of the now loosened covers and swing them over the side of the pallet.

Disaster. That's what this is.

I'm never having that much of that wine-like stuff again—that sweetness had it going down way too smoothly.

I get to my feet, feeling more in control now that I'm off the bed and upright.

Arawn stays sleeping, still not even close to waking.

Good.

These dragons sleep like rocks. Really giant ones.

I stare down at him, my eyes caressing the length of his impressive body. The smooth, sun-browned skin. The pretty scales. The rumpled length of his hair, smooth and shiny even now. My eyes slide down his muscled chest, his cobblestone abs...and stop at his navel.

The blankets just barely cover the promised land, shadows hinting at what's underneath, revealing only his hip and thigh on one side.

Yes, I imagine pulling it aside, but I don't do it, which I think earns me some major points.

Watching him for moments longer than I like—or would ever admit to—I stuff down the chaotic mix of feelings duking it out in my heart.

Stupid heart. Sometimes it just doesn't know what's good for it.

I find my dress in a small puddle on the floor and pull it on quickly, sliding my feet into the sandals I wear most days now because of the heat. Neither look any worse for wear. I smooth down my hair. There. Hopefully nobody will guess what might have happened judging from appearance alone.

I shake my head as I quickly leave a sleeping Arawn behind. Who am I kidding?

If anyone sees me right now, they'll know right away I'm engaging in the time-honored tradition of the Walk of Shame.

Luckily, it's early enough that I don't see anyone as I hurry out of Arawn's cave and down the path leading to the bottom of the valley. Hurrying over to the other side, I reach my cave and grab some clothes. I definitely need a bath.

Rushing out once more, I go to the small natural spring nearby and wash quickly, wincing a little at the soreness I find between my legs. But it's that delicious kind. The kind that leaves me feeling warm.

Another memory hits me. Of Arawn above me. Sliding slowly into me...

A flash of heat spears through me. Damn it!

Mentally shaking myself, I dry off and pull on the thin shirt and trousers that have become my everyday uniform. They help me beat the heat and remain fully mobile and functional to do everything I need to accomplish in a day.

I pull my wet hair up into a ponytail and shove my feet back into the simple, but comfortable sandals.

Feeling much more put together now that I'm clean and dressed normally, I wrap up my clothes into a small bundle and head back to my cave.

But I'm not as lucky on this trip as I was on the last. People are starting to trickle out to meet the day.

"Hey Fallon!" Delilah calls out. "Getting a head start today?"

I wave back at her and just smile awkwardly before ducking my head. I know from the heat rushing to my face that I'm blushing. I walk faster, not wanting to linger or be pulled into any conversation right now. I need time to get my mental game back together after the major mistake I just made. And time to process the fact that my body clearly wants to make that mistake again.

My head is down and I'm barreling forward with such determination that I almost don't stop in time when someone steps into my path. I stumble to a halt and look up automatically, an apology on my lips.

My heart stops.

Arawn.

The person I'm least prepared to see right now.

This meeting isn't at all like the lightness of the last time he blocked my path. He obviously came here specifically to see me. This isn't a route he would take very often, not when his cave is in the other section.

I clear my throat, fighting the urge to shuffle my feet like a guilty grade schooler.

"Good morning," I murmur lamely, not knowing how else to break the heavy silence between us.

"Good morning," he responds, his deep voice making my toes curl.

No, stop it toes! They aren't the only ones betraying me. My face feels like it's on fire, which means it must currently be a lovely shade of tomato red from embarrassment.

Arawn doesn't say anything else, his eyes searching mine.

I know he's about to bring up last night. I avert my eyes. I'm just not ready to talk about that yet. Honestly, I'll be ecstatic to never have it brought up.

"Uh, I have to go. Sorry," I mutter, peeking up at him quickly as I side step him on the path.

I see the hurt on his face briefly before he shuts it down.

It makes me feel like a real ass, but the guilt doesn't stop me from almost running away. And he doesn't try to block my path again, but just lets me leave. I find myself missing the playfulness he displayed earlier, when he tried to stop me multiple times.

But I suppress that response. This is for the best. If he was expecting something long-term, it's better he faces the reality now rather than later.

I don't want my very own dragon. I don't want romance, period. Even with one of the surviving human men. I don't want that kind of complication in my life. Simple is what I'm aiming for, and he just won't fit into that equation.

So, I try to put Arawn out of my mind as I first go to my cave to drop off my stuff and get my head together and then get started on my duties for the day. I'm not completely successful, but I do try.

When Kate asks if I can come with her and Errol to the city, I jump at the chance to escape the scene of the crime.

"Sure, I'll go get packed."

"Great—we'll meet you at the rover in fifteen."

Perfect. I get ready quickly and hurry over to the wall, where Errol and Kate are already waiting. This rover really is worth its weight in gold. Or whatever the equivalent of that would be here on Tajss.

The ride over to the city is quick and uneventful. I feel my shoulders dropping, relief flowing through me as we put distance between us and Arawn. I can't run from my problems forever. But I can for now, and I'm not above doing that. I'm only human.

When we arrive at the city, protected from the elements and the dangerous beasts that seem to run rampant here, Errol gets out and punches in the code to admit us.

The city is just as spectacular now as when I first saw it. Sure, it's not in perfect repair, a holdover from before what the Zmaj call the Devastation—the wars that decimated their society, sending them back thousands of years. But that doesn't take away from the impressiveness of it, of the architecture, the technology from the height of their civilization.

"Are you okay with heading over to one of the guest

apartments?" Kate asks as we exit the rover. "Rosalind wants to speak with us."

"Yeah, sure. I'll see you later."

I head over to the same building that I first stayed in here, the one Errol took us to. That feels like a lifetime ago now, though it really wasn't that long ago in terms of actual time, was it? Sometimes perception really is everything. I go to the same floor I stayed on then, figuring there will probably be an available apartment there. And it will be close to the others' places.

It'll be nice to catch up with the rest of our original group, those that decided to stay back in the city rather than come with Kate and me to Errol's little community in the cave system. I'm actually not in the empty apartment I find for very long. In fact, I'm just settling in when Kate and Errol show up.

"I figured you'd come back here," Kate says as they step inside after I open the door. "Can we speak to you real quick?"

"Sure."

It's not like I'm super busy. But I do feel a bit of concern at their quick arrival.

"What is this about?" I ask. "Is something wrong?"

"No," Errol reassures me. "We have been asked to go to the mining settlement."

"And I thought you would be a good person to take along," Kate adds. "If you want to come, of course. I can't guarantee that either the journey or our final destination will be a walk in the park."

"What is the trip for?" I ask.

"To check what they've culled from the mines," Errol explains. "This is what Rosalind wanted to speak to us about. And Kate is correct—we cannot guarantee the conditions. Though Bashir did successfully return from his own trip."

I smile at that. Why the hell not?

I haven't seen the mining settlement yet and this is the perfect opportunity to sate my curiosity. Not to mention that the timing is so damn convenient. Prolonging my separation from Arawn would be great. An excellent way to avoid the awkwardness. Maybe if I'm gone long enough, he'll go along with just ignoring what happened. A girl can hope.

"Sure," I agree. "Sounds interesting."

Kate grins and says, "That's one word for it. I, for one, hope it's real boring. I've had enough excitement for a lifetime."

She's not wrong about that.

"I hear you," I say sincerely.

"It is settled then," Errol announces, standing. "We will meet with Arawn tomorrow when he arrives and leave for the settlement shortly after."

"Arawn?" I ask, trying not to show my dismay at the mention of his name.

"He also volunteered to come with us," Kate explains. Maybe there's something on my face that gives me away because her look turns somewhat concerned. "Is that okay?"

"Yeah. Sure, yes," I say, trying out a smile that probably looks as fake as it feels. "I'll be ready to go. Tomorrow. With...all of you."

Smooth.

"All right," Kate agrees, but she doesn't look completely convinced.

Not surprising. It's the best I can do, though. I keep the smile on my face as they say their goodbyes and leave me alone again. But I drop it as soon as they're out of sight and lean my back against the closed door with a sigh. What are the odds? Why can't I just catch a break, damn it!

Why couldn't Errol or Kate have divulged the fourth member of our group before I agreed so quickly? I feel the urge to scream, but I keep it together. Barely. I'm an adult. I can do this.

And it isn't like I'm going to be alone with him. Kate and Errol will be there, and we'll be focused on our mission. It'll be fine. Really.

The little pep talk doesn't really do much for the pit in my stomach. Even my body doesn't believe me.

I take out my ponytail, running my hands through my hair in exasperation as I step away from the door. Now I'm going to have to face the dragon I've been so determinedly trying to sidestep. After drunkenly falling into bed with him on the heels of all the feels the mating ceremony gave me.

Real classy.

And needy.

How truly and completely embarrassing. How the hell am I going to keep him at bay when I apparently can't even suppress my own physical reaction to him whenever he simply enters a room?

"Why, Tajss, why?!" I ask dramatically, raising my hands up to the sky.

"Uh. I'll just come back later."

I look back to see Lanie backing out with her hands up. Great. Now she's going to think I'm unbalanced too.

"No, no, I'm fine," I reassure her, dropping my hands quickly. How embarrassing. Maybe that's becoming my brand.

She grins. "You sure?"

"Yeah. And it's good to see you."

"You too," she agrees, stepping into the hug, her hold just as firm as my own.

"Yeah, you have to tell us everything about the village," Addison pipes up from the open door.

"Yes, details please!" Ashlee agrees from just behind her.

I laugh, moving forward to hug them too, trying to act like everything is fine.

"Are you sure you're okay?" Lanie asks again, giving me a shrewd look. "You look a little..."

"Off," Addison finishes, exchanging a look with the other girls.

"No, no," I counter, trying really hard to make it believable. "I'm just a little tired."

"Uh huh," Ashlee says, not looking all that convinced.

I feel like the weight of my secret is pulling me down, like I'm sinking into the floor from it. But I really don't want to talk about it.

"I miss you guys," I try as they all settle down on the couch and chairs in the living area. "How have things been here?"

Come on. Let's just move on. There's a beat where I worry they're going to keep picking at me, but then Addison breaks the silence. My hero.

"Oh, man, the technology is so advanced!" Addison exclaims, leaning forward eagerly. "Maybe I can show you around later, so you can see what I'm talking about."

"That would be great."

"I've been working with Sarah's kedi—and I've actually seen more out there in the wild! They're so adorable and Picard is so smart—he learns faster than even a dog, I think," Lanie gushes.

"And we've made a lot of progress restoring the buildings, though it's slow work," Ashlee adds just as excited.

"I did notice the improvements when we came in," I say. "Impressive."

She beams at me. "It is, isn't it? Oh and we have so much more..."

The conversation flows easily between all of us, bonded as we are from our past experiences together.

I laugh and comment along with the rest of them, filling them in on the details of our life in the smaller group Kate, Nora, and I chose.

But though I have a wonderful time catching up, it still doesn't distract me completely. I just can't get my mind off of Arawn no matter how hard I try.

Not that I'll ever divulge that particular bit of information to anyone.

4

ARAWN

I feel a rush of anticipation as I arrive at the city. I just saw Fallon yesterday, but the cave system feels so empty without her there. I don't like not hearing her voice. Seeing her out and about doing her normal duties. And the fact that we still haven't reconnected after that night together makes me feel...unsettled. I need to see her.

However, my first stop needs to be to see Errol, to find out when we will be leaving. When I agreed to go on this trip to the mining settlement, I did not know that Fallon would be along for the trip as well. I cannot help but look forward to it more now, though I know the work we are going to do may not be the easiest or the simplest.

I find Errol easily enough—he and Kate usually stay in the same apartment when they come to the city.

"Was your journey safe?" he asks when he opens the door to me, clasping my arm warmly.

"Yes. How do you fare?"

"Well, well. But there is a slight delay—we will have to refuel the rover, and we also want to leave earlier in the day.

I believe we will be leaving tomorrow morning rather than starting our journey now."

I nod. It does make sense. It is much easier to see threats approaching when the suns are high in the sky to light our way.

"Good."

We chat a bit longer, but then Errol must excuse himself to deal with preparations for the trip. And I am free to track down my favorite prey.

It does not take me long to find where Fallon is staying in the city. I arrive just in time to find her and other females she is clearly familiar with stepping out of the building and into one of the nearby rooms where food is served.

So I slip inside after them.

I find the familiar pale, shining locks easily enough and make my way over to her table. The female sitting across from her widens her eyes as she sees me behind Fallon.

"Good morning," I murmur quietly.

I see Fallon's shoulders stiffen as she hears my voice. She turns her head slowly, angling it up so she can see me.

"Arawn," she says, surprise flashing across her face. "Good morning. Did you just arrive?" she asks politely.

I glance around the table. This polite version of Fallon must be because she is around her friends. I am willing to take advantage of that fact. A Zmaj uses all the tools at his disposal. If he is smart.

"Would you mind if I join you?" I ask, directing the question at the entire table rather than just Fallon.

"Of course!" the female across from Fallon agrees, the others chiming in after her.

"Here, you can sit next to Fallon," the female with her hair wrapped in two braids offers, getting up and moving aside.

"My thanks," I acknowledge as I take the seat.

Fallon opens her mouth to say something, but closes it

again without speaking. I keep my smile inside. I will take the small victory. So I sit down beside Fallon at the table and talk to her friends. All of them more welcoming than she, but she makes a valiant effort not to give away her feelings.

"Do you know a lot about kedis?" the female who gave up her seat for me, Lanie she is called, asks. "I've been working with them and learning about them, but I was just wondering if you've had any personal experience?"

"Ah. Yes, when I was young, there was a particular kedi that liked to follow me home..."

I regale the table with the story from my childhood, transitioning over to one about a hunt where a kedi was instrumental in my success.

"...and it ran right through the guster's legs, distracting it long enough that I was able to use my lochaber to kill it swiftly, before it was able kill my fellow warrior."

"Oh wow!"

"That's amazing!"

"I want a kedi now!"

I puff out my chest in pride at their responses and look out the corner of my eye to see Fallon's reaction. She does not look nearly as impressed as the others with my hunting prowess. Perhaps she is concealing her admiration as she concealed her reaction to my arrival from the others?

The food arrives as I worry at the problem, attempting different strategies to impress Fallon. But none seem to work.

And then the meal is over, and Fallon stands. "Come on guys, let's head out." She turns to me. "It was good to see you Arawn."

I nod, murmuring my goodbyes to the others as they also leave. Hmm. Fallon is a difficult one. But I will not cease my pursuit. Not when her actions earlier showed she feels the same desire for me that I feel for her. I simply have to help her acknowledge that fact. And to do that, I have to be in her vicinity. I nod to myself as I stand. That is settled then. I will endeavor to spend more time with her to help her see why she should desire me. So I make that my mission for the day.

I find her next at the market, where she wanders from stall to stall. But she is wily prey. When she sees me coming towards her, she ducks behind another stall, this one with many fluttering colorful fabrics that obscure her from my view. I hurry around the stall, but she is gone.

Vanished.

I smile.

Ah.

The female is an expert at evasion. But she forgets that even though I am a craftsman, all Zmaj males are hunters in our souls.

I feel the thrill of the hunt run through me as I walk through the market, careful to blend, to use cover. I find her again as she is speaking with another vendor, her eyes still looking around as she asks about a hat.

She does not expect me to appear from behind the vendor herself. Her eyes widen as I appear in front of her and sidle out to her side.

"Hello, Fallon."

"Hello," she murmurs, her jaw tight.

"You desire this hat?" I ask, gesturing to the female to hand it to me.

"No," Fallon murmurs. "Thank you," she adds, nodding at the other female as she turns to hurry away.

I do not bargain with the female for the hat, simply give her the asking price to secure it quickly. If Fallon desires the hat, I will procure it for her. I reach her quickly, my longer legs making quick work of the distance between us.

I set the hat upon her head. She glares at me.

"I said I didn't want it," she growls.

"Yes, however, I wanted you to have it," I coax. "I know your skin is delicate. Is more protection from the sun not good to have?"

She sighs, her glare fading.

"Thank you," she murmurs, softening slightly. "But I'm supposed to go meet with Addison now."

"I will walk you there," I say easily, keeping pace with her.

Rather than argue with me, she simply nods. And that is how the day continues. I happen upon her path throughout the daylight hours, despite her attempts to evade me. And I find myself having fun, enjoying the game of it. When I nonchalantly cross her path near the remnants of the central fountain, I relish the slight flush of exhaustion on her face at the game.

"Hello, Arawn," she greets me.

That is certainly an improvement. Perhaps I am slowly wearing down her resistance, so she will at least consider what is between us.

But I am wrong.

When the evening meal comes, I cannot find her anywhere, despite locating the other females she enjoys dining with.

"Where is Fallon?" I ask Lanie when I finally admit I will not find her myself.

"She wasn't feeling well so she stayed in her apartment," she explains. "Would you like to join us?"

"Thank you," I murmur, taking the seat she offers as my heart plummets at the news.

It seems as though Fallon has barricaded herself in her chambers. I do not believe she actually feels unwell. I am the reason she decided not to join the others for the meal. She seems quite dedicated to her avoidance of me.

"Is something wrong?" Addison asks, sharing a look with Lanie.

"No. I am simply pondering the upcoming journey we will be making to the mining settlement. Is there anything new you have heard of the place?"

I breathe a silent sigh of relief at successfully changing the subject as the two start to discuss the rumors swirling about the community that wants to keep their distance, despite the aid given to them.

Rather like a pouting child. Which, incidentally, is exactly how I feel at the moment. I thought Fallon was enjoying our game just as I was. But it is quite clear now that I was mistaken. She was genuinely attempting to avoid me.

The realization is...quite humbling. And it hurts. Feeling as though I need privacy to lick my wounds, I excuse myself as soon as the meal is over and go back to my own chambers. Sleep does not come easily despite the knowledge that I need to be at my best for the journey tomorrow. I finally do fall into a slumber, though when I wake, I do not feel all that rested.

That lack does not help my mood at all. Feeling sulky—a condition I have not felt since childhood long ago—I join Kate, Errol, and Fallon to pack up the rover Kate engineered.

It is a handy contraption indeed out in the desert, both increasing our swiftness and our safety with the metallic carapace we sit in. I can truly appreciate what feels like a luxury after traveling on wing and foot. It also means we will arrive at our destination relatively rested, which is good. I do not know exactly what we will find when we arrive.

"I already added the garbage. It's breaking it down and refueling," Kate explains as I carry out another heavy pallet of supplies to add to what we have already packed inside. "Fallon, could you show Arawn which of the packages we need to separate?"

Fallon nods, walking over to what has yet to be packed, not even sparing me a glance. I follow just as silently.

She hasn't said a word to me all morning. So I have followed suit. If she wishes not to engage, I refuse to keep chasing the interaction. Despite the ache in my chest.

She points out the packages and moves on to pick up some of the lighter items, still with no words. At one point while we are loading, she pushes a package towards me, and I acknowledge it with only a grunt. Somehow, we both manage to help pack the car without speaking to each other at all.

I see Kate and Errol exchange a look, so perhaps we are not being completely discreet about what is going on between us. Even as I see that, I do not attempt to engage with her. I have tried again and again to no avail. Perhaps I should attempt the opposite.

"We will eat breakfast and then we will begin the journey," Errol announces when we are done with the things we are taking.

Breakfast is more of the same. Fallon and I are both careful not to look at each other or interact directly as we eat. At this point, we are both almost completely silent, not even engaging in conversation with Kate and Errol.

The amused glint in Errol's eye now when he looks between the two of us confirms that they know something is going on between us. But the amusement tells me that he is mistaken as well.

Fallon has decided not to explore anything. This is not part of the beginnings of a mating.

Kate leans forward, towards Fallon.

"So, are you interested in getting some of the stuff they mined for yourself?" she asks, clearly trying to draw her into the conversation. Attempting to smooth things over, I believe.

"What do they have in the mines?" Fallon asks slightly grudgingly, her interest piqued.

"Oh, Arawn." Kate turns to me now. "I hear there is metal that is good for tech, but others that are good for jewelry and ornamental pieces. Do you know anything about that?"

It is a clear attempt to draw me into the conversation as well. But I am not so rude as to not answer, not when it is Kate and not Fallon attempting to pull me into speaking.

"Tajss has many types of metals, and I hear there is some variety in the settlement mines, but..."

I keep my answer short and concise, just as Fallon does. Between Kate's desire to have us join the conversation and our desire to be polite to her, we manage to have a stilted, dry back-and-forth that is almost more painful than the silence.

I shake my head as I continue to eat. This is not at all how I envisioned the beginning of this trip. It does not bode well for the rest.

5

FALLON

I slide a surreptitious glance over at Arawn's profile. Still just as stone-faced as he's been this entire trip. I look away again, before he can catch me looking at him. He really is angry. It's a little hard to get used to after the way he's been acting towards me so far. Playful, persistent. Always attentive, never masking how much he wanted me.

As contrary as it sounds after I've been actively avoiding him...I kind of miss that. I never claimed to be the most consistent person.

I turn to look out the window as the rover continues to eat up the distance between the city and the settlement. Kate talks quietly with Errol in the front as she drives us, but since my companion here in the back is beyond miffed with me, I've stayed mostly silent. It hasn't really helped the time pass any faster, that's for sure. Especially not combined with the blistering heat that feels like it's trying to bake us.

"God, I feel like I'm swimming in my own sweat," Kate mutters, pulling her shirt away from her chest, plastered there with the aforementioned sweat.

I hum my agreement, wrinkling my nose. It does feel like I just got out of a bath, but we haven't been anywhere near water. It's pretty gross. I guess I've gotten used to the cave system and then the city, where shade is abundant. Out here in the desert, even inside the rover, the heat is ridiculous. Like we're being baked in a tin can.

"Humans are not built for Tajss," Errol murmurs, tenderly pushing a lock of Kate's damp hair behind her ear. "Perhaps we will stop at the next oasis so both you and Fallon may use the water to lower your temperatures."

I sneak another look at Arawn. Cool as a cucumber. He doesn't even look uncomfortable. Well, not any more uncomfortable than sitting in this awkward silence could account for.

It's the same story when I look at Errol. He looks as comfortable as if he was sitting in a climate-controlled room with an icy cold drink in his hand. It's damned irritating. It's never been clearer to me that the Zmaj are adapted to thrive in this environment. And that we are not.

I sigh as I shift in my seat, even while I know trying to find a comfortable position while I'm this hot is a kind of fantasy in and of itself. I glance over at Arawn again. I really can't help it. When I look forward again, Kate is looking back at me through the rearview mirror, one eyebrow raised and a slight smirk on her face.

Busted.

Not that she hasn't already seen enough to know *something* is going on.

"A dip in an oasis does sound good," I comment, squinting my eyes out the window in the vain hope that maybe one will pop into existence if I just focus hard enough. And I'm trying to distract Kate from what she just saw.

"Agreed," Kate murmurs. "I'm willing to make do with a puddle if it's wet."

That startles a chuckle out of me, though the joke is only distracting for a moment. Groans and sighs abound, all from Kate and me as we continue the journey. Not surprising since we're also the only ones really suffering.

I cast another narrow-eyed look at Arawn. Sitting there, completely comfortable. With that beautiful, sharp jaw. That luxurious hair with those intriguing horns peeking through, those pretty, gleaming scales. His wings are tucked neatly against his back, his tail likewise neatly wrapped to the other side. Those truly impressive shoulders and that muscled body that clearly advertises the kind of strength his body contains...

I shift again in my seat, but this time because of a different kind of heat entirely. Somehow, it was easier to suppress those memories of that drunken night when he was still attempting to pursue me. Now that he isn't, now that he's choosing to be distant, which is what I wanted...

It's leaving too much room for me to remember. Remember the feel of his skin under my hands. The reverent look in his eyes when he touched me. The feel of his mouth... How completely encompassed I felt with him above me...

I grimace slightly as I shift again, another wave of heat passing through my body. How do I erase a memory that's so strong I can almost still taste Arawn on my lips? I have no idea. And being stuck in this car with him right beside me is no help at all. Damn it. Why did my critical mind have to take a vacation that evening?

My eyes clash with Kate's in the mirror again when I look away.

"Looks like you might be making your own puddle back there," she comments, wagging her eyebrows at me.

I feel myself flush a bright scarlet. "Kate!"

She winks back at me. Oh man, I want to just sink into

the ground and die. Do the men understand the joke? But my worries over whether or not Arawn and Errol understood Kate's meaning are pushed way into the background in the next instant.

"Kate." The warning in Errol's voice breaks right through my spiraling thoughts.

"I see them," Kate responds, her attention shifting instantly, her voice tense.

"See what?" I ask, trying to lean forward and look through the window.

I hear the high-pitched shriek before I see anything.

"Oh...shit."

It's a group of giant bird-like creatures, maybe six of them in total.

Their feathers are dark, ranging from gray to a deep blue, to an almost black.

Sharp, curved beaks look like they mean business, the razor-sharp claws adding to that impression.

"Tell me those things are vegetarians," I murmur.

"I'm afraid not," Kate responds grimly.

"They have targeted us," Arawn says quietly. He's leaned forward to look out the windshield as well, his eyes sharp, readiness emanating from him. "We will not be safe in the rover. Not with that many."

What?

"Yes," Errol agrees. "They could destroy it. Kate, stop the rover."

"Stop it?" she repeats incredulously. "Errol, there are six of those things! Six vtaks!"

"And two of us," Arawn inserts. "Fair odds," he adds with a grim, slightly reckless smile.

That look shouldn't be so hot.

"Kate, we will not survive if we keep driving. We cannot

go faster than they can fly," Errol says, his tone urgent. When I look out at the flock—is it still a flock if they're alien birds? —I can see he's right.

They're almost on top of us already.

Kate starts cursing as she slowly steps on the brake, slowing our forward momentum.

We aren't fully stopped before both Arawn and Errol grab their lochabers and leap out of the car.

"Fallon—get the poles!" Kate orders as she steps harder on the brake, bringing the rover to a rocking halt. "Hurry!"

The poles!

I immediately twist in my seat and grab the cool metal of one, threading it through the seats to Kate in the front before grabbing another myself.

Thanks to Penelope's survival book and our interest in never being sitting ducks again, one of the things we decided to create were these metal poles with sharp ends, fashioned for guarding and defense.

I'm guessing these birds aren't proof against a good old stabbing.

Heart pounding, I slide out of the rover right behind Kate, intent on fighting rather than just sitting and hoping not to die.

I've done too much of that.

My eye immediately goes to Arawn, reassuring myself he's still well. An uncomfortable thing to realize, but there it is.

Luckily, he's leaping through the air, hale and healthy, his lochaber swinging powerfully as he cuts through the wing of one of the birds, sending the powerful creature careening to the ground. Wow. I don't have time to dwell on his show of prowess though. Not with what feels like a hundred birds shrieking above us, even though I know it's only five.

"Fallon—watch out!" Kate shouts.

I let myself stare too long at Arawn. I grip the pole and turn to look, but the vtak is closing in too fast, its sharp claws extended, shining menacingly in the sunlight.

I start to duck and bring up the pole, but I feel like I'm moving through molasses, my muscles feeling as though they're responding at a snail's pace.

Slow.

Too slow.

It'll reach me long before I can do anything about it, and those claws will slice me into ribbons. I don't give up even as I think it, but I know in my bones that I'm right. But I am not going to go down cowering. I brace myself for the impact, trying to decide how best to do damage once I'm hit.

But the impact never comes.

Something plows into the giant bird's side so fast and hard that I hear the crunch of bone. I whirl around as time snaps back into place, my pole coming up in a defensive stance. Just in time to see Arawn flip his lochaber and bring it down hard on the wounded vtak's skull, cracking through it in one hard blow. I gape at him, even as he pulls his lochaber free.

He pauses to give me one swift glance. To make sure I'm not hurt? Before I can be sure, he leaps up into the air once more, his wings flaring for lift, his tail snapping out behind him.

"Stay alert!" he orders.

Right.

Alert.

Shaking off my shock, the undeniable warmth at his fierce show of protection, I resolutely turn my attention back to the sky. I can't let that happen again.

The next time one of the birds targets me, I stab upward with all of my strength, crouching down to avoid it and to stabilize my body. The tip doesn't pierce its underbelly that time. It flaps its wings hard, rising up to avoid much damage.

Then Arawn is there again, tearing into the thing with a vengeance. Maybe it's stupid, but I'm not as scared as I should be. I can feel Arawn's eyes on me the whole time. And I know he'll intervene if I'm in danger. I can feel something in me soften towards him, but I don't have time to examine it in the melee.

Errol watches Kate with just as much focus as Arawn watches me, shoving her out of the way of a swooping vtak, its sharp claws extended with clear intent. The thing doesn't stand a chance when Errol leaps onto its back at the bottom of its flight path.

I shift my attention away as I see movement nearing me. All right, here we go again. Crouching down, I try my method once more, stabbing up with a yell as the creature nears.

Second time is the charm. I feel the tip punch through the feathers and then the body underneath with a grim sense of satisfaction. The bird shrieks even louder above me, flapping its wings hard in an attempt to get away. Hard enough that my feet start to lift from the ground.

"Got you!"

Kate's arms wrap around my waist and together, we pull down hard to free up my pole, managing to tear a gash through the vtak. It tries to fly off, but it's gushing blood and other things now as it wobbles through the air. Its wings start to falter, its height falling rather than rising.

"It is done."

I turn back at Arawn's deep voice, my chest heaving, sweat pouring off of me.

"What?" I ask.

But when I turn around, I realize he is directing his words to Kate. My heart clenches.

"That vtak will die in moments," he says, jerking his head towards the one Kate helped me with. "And the others are already dead." His eyes shift towards me. Do they soften somewhat or is that just wishful thinking? They turn back to Kate almost immediately. "We may put down our weapons now."

Only then do I realize that I still have it up in the air as if anticipating another attack. I nod, slowly lowering, feeling the adrenaline still pumping through my body.

He turns away, still not looking directly at me. Even though it's clear that last bit was for me. Nobody else had their weapons up and ready anymore.

"We will cut up the meat and set it on a fire," he announces.

"What?" Kate asks, turning to look at Errol. "We don't need more food. We have enough rations."

"We do not waste meat," Errol responds. "And more food will not hurt where we are going. We will cook the vtaks." He grins. "And I think it fitting that we celebrate our victory in the traditional manner—where the felled predators become the meat of their intended prey." Reaching out, he pulls Kate close. "You fought valiantly, my mate. As did you, Fallon," he adds nodding at me.

Kate looks over at me, shrugging slightly. This is clearly some kind of masculine, Zmaj thing. A tradition there is no use fighting against. Besides, they're right. It seems like a waste to leave food behind.

So we all get to work with our own knives, hacking away at the still-warm bodies. I remember a time where I didn't know how to field dress an animal. I wipe some of the blood onto the feathers in front of me. Feels like a lifetime ago now.

Arawn works alongside me, Errol and Kate obviously together. But he still says nothing, his face closed off as his hands move competently, efficiently. I'm okay. But he's obviously been doing this his whole life.

I bite my lip as I keep cutting up the meat into manageable chunks. He's...still not speaking to me. And it somehow hurts more now.

We finish breaking down the meat and Errol and Arawn set it onto a large fire, careful to not get it so close that it'll burn. And Arawn still doesn't say a word to me. Someone would have to be both deaf and blind not to notice, and Errol and Kate are neither. I appreciate that they don't bring it up though. As I sit down and watch the flames, it's a bitter truth I ruminate over.

"I believe there are some caverns we can take shelter in nearby," Arawn murmurs to Errol. "It is not a good idea to keep traveling so close to night."

Errol nods.

"Can you go scout them?"

Arawn nods, standing.

"I will be back shortly."

I feel a pang of fear as he goes off alone. Which is stupid. He obviously knows quite well how to take care of himself—and me. The way he rushed over and saved me during that fight... I'd be lying if I didn't admit it affected me. Unlocked something deep and primitive inside me that I didn't even know was there. Something my defensive mind can't just explain away.

And I can't deny that when Arawn returns less than five minutes later, I feel a rush of relief. Oh, man. I have it bad.

I watch him as we eat, trying not to be obvious about it but unable to stop myself even if Errol and Kate can see. Heck, even if Arawn notices, really.

When he's still silent after we pack up the meat and trudge over to the caverns, it stings. No, it burns. And as we settle in for the night in the relative safety of a small cavern, I can't escape the thought that I did this. Messed up what was between us. Started this silent feud to push him away.

I turn over restlessly. The ground is hard under my thin pallet.

But I know that isn't what keeps me awake.

6

ARAWN

J stare up at the cavern ceiling, watching as the early morning light slowly starts to seep in. I thought perhaps moving to a separate cavern from Fallon would help. Escaping the sight of her, her ever maddening scent. The feelings she invokes without even trying.

But it did not help me much. I was restless all night even alone in this cavern. My body hard and aching with thoughts of Fallon. My thoughts about her refusing to settle down so I could sleep.

My hearts are bereft, set adrift in the wilderness she cast me into after our drunken mating. Does she not understand the import of that night? Does she feel nothing that she could cast me aside so easily the next morning and mean it? Have I been living in a dream believing that I can win her heart in return?

Perhaps she really does feel nothing for me. I feel a sharp stab of pain at that thought but force myself to examine it anyway, rather than burying it as I have the urge to. If she feels nothing and refuses to allow me to attempt to win her...

What can I do?

What recourse do I have?

I smell her scent even now, as though my mind cannot let go of her even when we are physically separated. It is unfair that I am forever plagued with thoughts of her while she seems not to care—

There! The scrape of a foot against stone.

I sit up and turn to the entrance of the small cavern I traveled to in the night. My pulse immediately starts to increase as I see the focus of my thoughts, her pretty, bright hair backlit by the sunlight, creating a halo to frame her face. The face that never leaves my thoughts no matter how much I try to cast it out.

She stops as I turn my attention to her, looking at me somewhat hesitantly before taking another step inside. Another step closer.

"Good morning," she begins, clearing her throat. Is she nervous? "Would you like some water?" she asks, extending her canteen.

My hands clench at my sides as I resist the urge to reach for her rather than the water she offers.

Yes, she is warmer towards me since the vtak attack. After I protected her. But that does not mean that she desires more from me than that protection. Perhaps this is simply a show of gratitude.

"Thank you," I murmur, reaching out to take the vessel from her. It is not what I want to do, but it is all I allow myself. I take a few sips, not needing nearly as much water to survive here on Tajss as the humans need, wasting it as they do through their skin when they overheat.

"We're setting off in an hour," she informs me. "Errol is asking for your help in packaging some of the meat. We can't take all of it, so we will have to leave the rest for the beasts.

He's also suggesting we ask Rosalind for scrap metal, so we can attach a wagon to the rover, too. It would make transporting things like this a lot easier."

I hand her the water as I rise to my feet.

"Not a bad idea," I acknowledge, leaning down to quickly roll up my pallet.

I don't want to continue our conversation only to be hurt again when she does not return my affection, so I nod at her and leave the cavern, my things neatly packed. Surprise crosses her face at my abrupt exit, but it does not stop me.

I would be lying to myself if I denied the fact that even this small overture from her has left me with a warm glow inside.

Being woken by the woman who seems able to reach into my soul, to make a home for herself there with a mere glance...it is something I did not even know I craved until now. But I do not trust it. Perhaps if it had happened earlier. How can I trust any gesture now, when she ran from me after so much more? When she was able to shut me out after what we shared that night?

I sigh. No, it is better to maintain a distance. No matter how painful it is to do so. How wrong it feels. I walk out of the cavern and use my wings to help travel the short distance from the cavern to the kill site, my feet barely touching down on the sand between long leaps.

We already did the majority of the work the day before, but there is still more that needs to be done before we can leave. Kate and Errol are already hard at work, Kate carefully wrapping the meat for transport and Errol continuing to cut and collect it.

"Arawn, could you help me with packaging the meat and stacking it in the rover?" Kate asks when she sees me.

"Of course," I agree immediately.

So I make my way over to her and take the bigger cuts of meat, wrapping them in the durable guster skin we keep on hand whenever possible. I know the rover contains many such skins for exactly this reason. Wasting meat is simply not done.

When Fallon arrives, she walks over to Errol, helping him cut and collect. I do not look directly at her, but my awareness of her seems like it will never diminish. When she is in the vicinity, a part of me focuses on her and only her. I look up as she arrives with another cut of meat, taking it from her with a nod but not acknowledging her otherwise.

When she walks away once more, Kate makes a small sound.

I look over at her.

"Is something amiss?" I ask, frowning.

She sighs, continuing to wrap the meat she has in front of her.

"I just...I think you need to know a little more about Fallon's background to understand her. Understand why she is the way she is."

"Her background?" I ask, curious. "What about her past do you believe I should know?"

Kate looks over at Fallon. Gauging how far away the other female is?

"Fallon's childhood...it wasn't exactly idyllic," she starts, not looking at me as she continues to work. "Her father wasn't an easy man. He expected a lot from her from a very young age and didn't give a lot back in return."

"What did he expect from her?" I ask, feeling a stirring of anger. I do not like thinking of Fallon being harmed when she was young and vulnerable. Open to hurt.

"He expected her to work hard always. To be perfect in school, to never be in trouble. To do everything without

67

complaint. Even when she was a small child, and she fell or sustained all the other small wounds children often do, he never gave her a hug or told her he loved her. Like she was a robot who didn't have feelings. One that was only created to work efficiently." Kate's lips compress into a thin line, obviously as disturbed by that line of thought as I am hearing it. "Some people simply aren't meant to be parents." She glances over at me. "Anyway. I just thought you should know."

It is apparently quite clear there is something between Fallon and me, if Kate has decided to tell me this important bit of information. And since I obviously need help, I can only be grateful that Kate has decided to intervene in this small way.

"My thanks," I murmur, wrestling with the emotions the concise story has drawn from me.

I look over at Fallon, her face flushed with the heat as she continues to work quickly alongside Errol.

From Kate's own observations, Fallon's father was a hard man with little empathy. I do not doubt her assessment. Kate is not someone prone to exaggeration, not like this. If what she said is the case, Fallon had a difficult parent, indeed. I try to imagine her as a small child, try to imagine how she must have felt being raised so coldly. Children need discipline, yes. But they also need room to make mistakes, need softness and love to grow into strong, resilient adults.

Now that I know what her childhood must have been like, I can see the scars of it in her now. The hard shell that she shows the world. Her resistance to connect past a certain point. She is protecting herself. Protecting a heart that was bruised too much when she was too young to defend herself properly.

This changes things. Kate was right to tell me this.

My approach was not the right one for someone carrying emotional wounds such as this. But perhaps I could attempt a different approach now. A different manner in which to share my own now slightly hesitant self. I might be hurt again.

The question is, is Fallon worth the risk? Despite the wounds she's dealt me, the answer is quick and sure.

Yes. She is more than worth the risk. I simply need to show her that I am not her father. That I will only treat her with care, that I value all of her. That I care how she feels, what she thinks. That I see her as a full person.

I ruminate on my new approach as I move my hands automatically. We do not talk much more as we finish packing the meat quickly and efficiently, not wanting to waste daylight any more than necessary.

But after we clean off and sit inside the rover, I look over at Fallon next to me.

It is my turn to make an overture. She extended her hand already, whether it was in gratitude or something more.

"Did you sleep well last night, Fallon?" I ask, beginning with something neutral and easy.

She glances over at me, clearly startled at the question. I have been punishing her with distance. But was that wise when that punishment was also hurting me?

"Oh, well, yes," she stumbles through. "How about you? Why did you move to a different cavern?"

Is there a hint of pain in her voice? Or am I simply hoping it is there, that she missed my presence as I missed hers?

"I was restless and did not want to wake any of you." Only partially true. "I did not sleep well. But that was simply because I had other matters on my mind."

"I understand that," she murmurs.

Perhaps she does.

"What were those poles you and Kate used when we were attacked?" I ask, wanting to keep our conversation going.

Fallon flashes a grin at me, her green-blue eyes sparkling.

I feel that look jolt through my body, and I know I would do many things to see it again. To see her joyful. Happy.

"Oh, we had those made after reading Penelope's survival book. We've been just prey here on Tajss for too long and wanted a way to fight back." She shrugs. "We're obviously not as strong or as good in a fight as you guys, but at least we aren't just waiting to be saved or killed."

I nod, impressed at the ingenuity. The poles give them reach and would be useful against many kinds of creatures. They chose their weapons well.

"I understand. And both you and Kate were a help in the fight." It is true. I was surprised by how effective the two of them were.

"That's generous of you to say," she responds with a chuckle. "But I know you had to keep an eye on me the entire time."

I nod, remembering the terror inside me as I saw Fallon in harm's way more than once. It is not something I particularly want to repeat.

"Even still," I murmur. "You were not easy prey. And you and Kate were able to kill one of the vtaks on your own. Impressive by any standard."

"It was, wasn't it?" she says, a hint of excitement in her voice. "We're going to have to tell the girls when we get back —they'll be beyond excited to hear the poles actually work!"

I laugh at her enthusiasm as we continue to speak. The conversation actually starts to flow easily now that we are both trying. The rest of the ride to the mining settlement passes much more smoothly than the time in the rover so far this trip. The air between Fallon and me is infinitely less tense, though I can also feel how careful both of us are being with the other. That is fine. This is a start and I am more than happy with that. We have time to learn to be more comfortable in each other's company.

"There is the New Village," Errol announces after some time.

"And there's the welcoming party," Kate adds wryly. "Don't look all that welcoming, do they?"

I look out the front of the rover and see what she is commenting on. The New Village is neither like the Tribe's cave system or like the city. It was built neat and tidy at one point, with public squares and functional buildings, but it was never the high-tech marvel of the city. And it does not have the sturdiness of the natural cave system we live in. It is more vulnerable in every way, but it is still a very large step above having to create something from nothing.

Currently, the New Villagers are waiting just outside their settlement, obviously having spotted us coming from some distance. They do not look at all welcoming, just as Kate noted. At least they have the good sense to have people looking out for threats.

Kate stops the rover with a good distance between the crowd and us. A wise precaution.

"Here we go," she murmurs as one of the human men steps towards us. "Showtime."

"Let us meet him on our feet," Errol says in a low voice.

I murmur my agreement, following him out of the rover. Kate and Fallon step out after us. I resist the urge to tell them to go back into the relative safety of the vehicle. If the group is physically threatening in any way, I know that Errol and I are more than a match for them. And I do not want to undermine either Kate or Fallon's authority in front of these strangers.

The man who stepped in front of the group gives both Errol and me a wary look. This must be Jackson. I was told he was the leader here, though I was also told he had some strong opposition against him in his own group. So a leader, but not one on completely sturdy ground. That is good information to have. An insecure leader is often more volatile and dangerous then one settled into his role.

"What brings you here?" he asks, his tone as unwelcoming as his face. He gives Errol and me another sweeping glance. "This is a human-only settlement," he adds.

How charming.

But I knew before we came that this settlement contains the remnants of Gershom's followers, those that never wanted to work with the Zmaj. Never mind the fact that we are so much better adapted to Tajss and are the reason the humans were able to survive here when they arrived.

In my experience, there is no real reasoning with people who are behaving in a manner that is not logical in the first place. That is likely why Rosalind has resorted to simply sending aid and hoping they will see the error of their ways. I understand bribery, but I also wonder if allowing these people to truly be on their own for a long period of time wouldn't expedite this process. It is difficult to hold on to hate as a group if your bellies are empty.

"We are here on Rosalind's behalf," Errol announces in a clear voice.

The words send a ripple through the crowd, setting off a lot of murmuring as the people look at each other.

"Are you?" Jackson asks, still suspicious.

I understand his wariness when it comes to safety. Leading a group means being careful. More careful than if you were only responsible for yourself. But it does not mean being hostile. Not when those arriving could be there to help, like we are. Another example of hate getting in the way of what these people actually need. I do not know how much respect I can have for a leader who does not always put the needs of his people first. It is his job to steer them in the correct direction.

"Yes," Kate says, ensuring everyone assembled hears her as well. "I have a note signed by both Rosalind and Sarah."

That sends an even larger reaction through the crowd as Kate steps forward with a missive in her hand, Errol keeping step with her. He would never leave his mate vulnerable near potentially hostile people. Jackson takes the note cautiously. The crowd watches as he unfolds it, reading the contents silently.

More than a few keep their eyes trained on Errol and me, suspicious that we are a threat. We could be a threat, so I do not take that suspicion to heart.

I watch Jackson's reaction with the rest, though he is careful not to show much through his expression.

I know everyone here knows Rosalind, but they trust Sarah more.

A dark-haired woman steps to Jackson's side, looking over his shoulder.

"What does it say?" she asks in a low voice.

Jackson looks up. "That they're here to see what progress we've made with our mine." The hostility from the crowd sharpens noticeably. "And that they've brought supplies for us as well."

The hostility shifts once more, this time to something slightly softer.

I am glad we brought food. Without the bribe, I do not feel we would have gotten much farther than this. Though it is still obviously a sensitive situation.

I hear the mutters from the crowd.

"They're just here to steal what we've worked so hard for."

"Do they think they can control us so easily?"

"Jackson can't let them in. That would be..."

It is clear Jackson hears the negative murmurs as well.

But there are also those who are looking back at the rover

73

curiously. Perhaps because of the vehicle itself. But I am guessing also because they want to see what we have brought for them.

I know they must still have some food left—Rosalind gave them enough to last—but they must be watching the stores dwindle. And worrying.

Jackson considers us as he tucks the note into his pocket. Refusing us would be...unwise. Rosalind has a lot more at her disposal than the villagers here do, both in terms of supplies and in terms of force. Humans are simply no match to the Zmaj when it comes to physical prowess. They cannot even properly hunt their own meat here on Tajss.

I know for a fact that the villagers here only survive because Rosalind has been sending aid to them. They could not have fed themselves otherwise. What bargaining power can a group really have if they are so dependent? I know all of that. But I still wait, not knowing what he will decide.

And what will we do if he does refuse? Do we not give them the supplies? Do we go to the mines without their permission? Simply turn around and report back to Rosalind? Luckily, we do not have to make any of those difficult choices.

"Well. Then I suppose we shall allow you to stay here as our guests." He smiles, though there is no true humor or welcome in it. "Temporarily, of course."

"Of course," Kate agrees politely, her voice just as warm as his. Which means not at all. "Thank you for your hospitality."

The edge in the air means I do not relax my guard even though Jackson has agreed to allow us in. I do not trust the control he has over his people, even if I had not heard of the power struggles occurring within the settlement. I make sure to stay near Fallon.

Errol gestures to the rover.

"Perhaps your people would like to help unload the

supplies? We have meat that has been smoked and prepared to weather the seasons, as well as fresh vtak meat that should be eaten first."

"Vtak?" Jackson asks.

"We were attacked by those giant birds on the way here," Kate explains. "So now they're food."

People exchange glances, clearly impressed. They must have encountered the birds at some point.

Jackson nods, turning to give out orders to a small group of people who immediately make their way over to the rover. Kate leads them to the back and directs them as to what to take.

I can see the people eyeing the rover itself as well. I understand. The vehicle is arguably more valuable than the food, especially for miners like them. I can only guess they are thinking of how much easier transporting ores would be with a vehicle such as this. But stealing it would be difficult, unless they manage to take the key and the code from Kate, which I sincerely doubt she will give up unless under extreme pressure.

"My people will make use of the meat," Jackson says after we close up the rover. "Come. We are about to have our communal meal. I suppose you are hungry as well after your trip."

"We are. Our thanks," Errol answers for us.

I would rather not eat with people so hostile, but I also know separating ourselves immediately will not endear them to us. So we follow Jackson through the crowd and into the small village.

It looks somewhat worse for the wear. From the dents and damage, I can only surmise the abandoned town was hurt even further by the meteorite showers we have been having recently.

We are led over to a square where food is being prepared.

It is obviously from the last shipment that Rosalind sent over to them, but those preparing it still hand us plates begrudgingly. Even though we also just brought them several more months' worth of food to live on.

I do not understand this level of ungratefulness, but we are not here to understand these people. We are here to lend a helping hand and see what progress they have made in the mines. So our mission is not completely altruistic. Though I doubt they would be more welcoming even if it was.

Errol and I stay near Kate and Fallon the entire time we eat, watching everyone while we do so.

If it would not have been rude, I would not have eaten the food they gave us for fear it was poisoned. The fact that it all came from one communal pot, all made for everyone, is the only thing that does not have me refusing for us anyway.

As soon as we are finished with the meal—which we ate in near silence, Jackson watching us but not bothering with even small talk—we are led over to our rooms.

Or our shared rooms.

There are two small buildings side by side that they have allocated for us, both of them basically having one usable room.

"We have two rooms for you," the man who Jackson assigned to us informs us. "You can decide to bunk how you want," he adds, casting a judgmental stare at both Kate and Fallon, as if they are beneath him for consorting with Zmaj.

I wonder if he understands either Errol or I could break him in half without any strain. Perhaps he would be less openly hateful if he did know.

But we are here to build open lines of communication, not alienate these people further.

Unfortunately.

"Thank you for your help," Kate says coolly. Dismissively.

The man hesitates, but then nods and turns to leave.

By silent agreement, we remain quiet until he is out of range.

"What an asshole," Fallon murmurs, shaking her head.

"We're probably going to have to deal with a lot of that while we're here," Kate points out, her tone resigned. "It's like they can't help themselves. Even though they know they need us, need the help Rosalind provides."

"Idiocy is not something that can be easily remedied," Errol agrees, looking around the room we find ourselves in.

The accommodations leave much to be desired.

There is one thin pallet on the ground and the windows are broken.

If the room was cleaned since the New Villagers first moved here, I do not see much indication of that.

"Do you guys want this room or the other equally unimpressive one we saw before?" Kate asks as she glances around. "Aren't we spoiled for choice?"

Fallon glances over at me and then away again.

"Either is fine," she murmurs, not arguing about how we are dividing up our group.

It only makes sense that Errol would be with his mate.

Errol nods.

"Why do you not remain here? Kate and I will go to the room he showed us first."

I nod as Fallon murmurs her agreement.

"It's decided then. We'll see you in the morning," Kate says, hugging Fallon before stepping away hand in hand with Errol. "I'm beat. At least we're under a roof. Shout if you need us—I'm sure we'll be able to hear you. We have a matching broken window," she observes with humor.

Fallon chuckles.

"All right. Same goes for you guys."

They nod, and with one final wave, leave us, closing the door gently behind themselves.

Closing us into the relative quiet.
Alone.
In our shared space.
I feel nerves and hope rise inside me.
Perhaps this is just the chance I need with Fallon.

7

FALLON

*W*ell, this is awkward. I didn't expect to be thrown right into the deep end with Arawn like this. We'd only just started speaking to each other again in something resembling normal conversation and now we have to share a room. We don't even have the buffer of Errol and Kate to lessen the tension between us. Not ideal.

"You can layer your pallet over the one given," Arawn says.

"Huh?"

I turn to him, still somewhat lost in my thoughts about the subject.

"The pallet," he repeats, gesturing to the meager sleeping pad. "You could put yours over it and have two layers."

I frown down at the hard floor. Sand is definitely more forgiving than the stone that is made of.

"What about you?"

He shrugs, turning towards the other side of the room.

"I will set my pallet down here." He glances at me over his shoulder. "Do not worry—I am accustomed to much harsher conditions than this."

"Aren't we all," I mutter, eliciting a quick grin from him. "Thank you."

He nods but doesn't make a fuss about it.

I start to unpack my things, shaking out the pallet that is on the floor before I place my own on top of it. I wouldn't trust the thing enough to lie down on it directly, but it does add a nice cushion between my own pallet and the floor.

A slide a glance over to Arawn as he lays his own down. He is such a gentleman. I never thought I would use that word to describe him, but it fits. Maybe that playfulness that I'm starting to miss distracted me enough that I didn't notice the core goodness of him. Now that he isn't crowding my feelings anymore, and we're speaking again, I can see just how considerate he is. How...sweet.

His eyes meet mine when he looks over, but I don't look away in embarrassment. Not this time.

"I am curious," he starts softly as he settles down to sit on his pallet. "How was life on your ship in comparison to life here on Tajss? I know Tajss is hard, but what was the biggest adjustment you needed to make when your people crashed here?"

I switch gears mentally, surprised at the incisive question. I can see from the intent look in his eyes, from the way he focuses on me, that he really wants to know. So I give it real thought.

"The first thing we felt was the heat," I admit, thinking back to the sharp fear of the unknown when we first landed on this planet. Knowing we had nowhere else to go anymore. "The ship's climate was always controlled, obviously, so it was always at a pleasant seventy degrees." I shake my head. "I never felt heat like this before, unless it was coming from an oven while we were cooking food," I chuckle.

Ah, seventy degrees. It sounds amazing.

"I can see you are not adapted to suffer the heat here," Arawn agrees. "For one, your people are always wet."

"Wet?" I repeat, startled. Then I have to laugh as I realize he means we're sweaty. "Oh, you must mean how we sweat in the heat. I've gotten a lot better since we started taking epis. But I bet it's pretty gross for you guys, huh?"

They never sweat. They're obviously built to conserve water, which makes sense in a place like this. I could only imagine what they might think of the fact that our skin is often sweaty when they look perfectly pristine. He shakes his head.

"I do not find the sweat repulsive," he disagrees. "Only different," he finishes, his eyes sliding over me.

Even if I wasn't inclined to believe him, the heat in his eyes when he looks at me would have convinced me otherwise. It might be enough to make me start to sweat all on its own. I resist the urge to fan myself at that look.

"And the lack of water, the sameness of the desert is a lot to take in. Though I guess the ship was a lot of the same too." I think back to the initial landing. And the horror we faced too soon after. "And the creatures here, of course," I add seriously. "We lost quite a few people to the guster before Gomul swooped in to save us."

He nods, his eyes somber as well.

"And that is why you all decided to fashion those sharp poles," he murmured. "So as not to be so vulnerable again."

I nod, smiling slightly. If nothing else, the poles offer some mental comfort.

"Yeah. I know we aren't anywhere in the same league as you guys, even with the weapons, but I definitely felt less vulnerable with one of them during the vtak attack. I'm definitely taking them on any trip I end up going on."

"Do not belittle yourself so. You fought valiantly when the beasts descended from the air."

My smile turns into a real one at the sincerity in his voice. The admiration. It warms something deep inside me to hear that from him. I know I'm not his peer, at least not when it comes to physical prowess, but I appreciate the acknowledgment, appreciate that he makes me feel like an equal in this way. He clearly outmatches me in physical strength and ability, but I firmly believe it's never a good idea to discount a strong warrior spirit, which I know I have. One that has been tempered by life.

As we continue to talk, I feel myself relaxing, opening up to him. And I feel him doing the same, warming up to me in a way that's different from before, on a level deeper than that first initial physical attraction. It's something I honestly wasn't expecting, but it's really nice.

"Are you hungry?" Arawn asks as night starts to settle in.

My stomach growls before I can answer.

"It was kind of difficult to eat much of anything with everyone glaring at us," I admit sheepishly.

He nods, smiling slightly.

"Just so. Wait here—I will go find food for us."

"That would be great—are you sure you don't need help?"

He shakes his head.

"I will be back momentarily."

And then he's gone. All right. Guess I'll just lie here and wait. Not a bad outcome.

He's back within fifteen minutes, but he doesn't come into the room right away. I hear him moving things around just outside the door and sit up.

At least I think it's him. A little more concerned at that thought, I climb to my feet and creep over to the door. If the welcoming party hadn't been so hostile, maybe I wouldn't immediately start thinking it might be someone up to no good, but there you go.

I open the door just a crack, slowly so as to not make a

sound. When I peek out through the narrow opening, I see something I could never have predicted. It is Arawn. But he's not coming in for a reason.

I watch as he places flowers on a large stone, flat enough to double as a table which is obviously his intention as he settles food and plates on it for us, a thick squat emergency candle set there as well, lit and ready to go. I feel my stomach clench at the sweet scene. I take it all in warily, feeling myself tense up again. This looks a heck of a lot more romantic than I'm comfortable with.

Is he expecting more to come out of this sleeping arrangement than just talking? Because, honestly, that's all I feel up for.

"Fallon," Arawn murmurs, spotting me when he turns. I jump a little, feeling slightly guilty for watching without him knowing. "Come—I wanted us to be able to eat outside where it is less..." He struggles for a word.

"Depressing?" I finish for him, smiling despite myself as I open the door wide.

He sighs, nodding.

"Yes, depressing," he agrees. "This is the best I could assemble for us. I miss the communal meals with the Tribe."

I feel my shoulders drop a little at that. Communal meal. I look at the table again and relax a bit more. Yeah, it looks romantic. But now that he brought up the communal meals, I can get the vibe he was going for.

"It's lovely," I say, touched at the effort he put in for us. "Thank you."

He smiles, gesturing to the smaller rocks he's arranged on either side to be our seats.

"Please, take a seat," he murmurs.

I nod, gingerly sitting down on the hard rock. It isn't terrible, but it does bring home the fact that we aren't welcome guests here.

Despite Arawn's excellent efforts. At least I'm relaxed enough to actually eat now that the New Villagers aren't glaring at us, ready to pick apart any word we might say.

We've been banished to the edges of the village, so I'm not that worried that people will hear us either, though I suppose it would be prudent for Jackson to have someone watching us while we're here. Just in case, I keep my voice low, as does Arawn.

"We do not know whose ears are nearby," he murmurs when he notices me matching his decibel level. I nod. But then we don't speak of it again, moving on to topics that won't be an issue even if people do overhear.

"Did you ever see this settlement before the Devastation?" I ask, looking around at it.

It gives me the same feeling as the city does. Probably because it was obviously built well but has been worn down by time and lack of maintenance. Though the New Village has also been battered by the meteorite showers without the benefit of the shield the city has on line.

Arawn shakes his head.

"Not this particular mining settlement, no," he says. "But I have seen others before. The metals that can be found here on Tajss can be quite precious, a valuable commodity."

I nod.

"I'm guessing there must be a good amount here, or there was at some point, if they went through all the trouble of building this place."

"Yes, this is a fair assessment..."

We speak about the village, about the mines. Then we talk about the journey here before switching back to the city and how it used to be before the Devastation. The topics flow, one into another, with Arawn asking me questions about the ship, about the tunnels, even as I ask him about Tajss.

To my surprise, I don't even realize hours have passed until Arawn looks up at the sky.

"Perhaps we should be retiring," he says reluctantly. "Tomorrow will likely be a full day."

I nod, feeling a surprising stab of disappointment. I was having fun. Arawn is a surprisingly good conversationalist. I feel a twinge of guilt at that thought. Perhaps he always was, and I just wrote him off as a boneheaded alpha male without giving him a chance. I'm learning a lot more about him on this trip than I expected to.

"Thank you for dinner, Arawn," I murmur.

Then I do something I've been wanting to do all throughout the night. Maybe it isn't a smart move, but...

I lean forward, across the stone acting as a table, but pause a few inches away from Arawn's lips, wanting to give him a chance to pull back if he wants to. I wouldn't blame him, not after how I behaved the last time we were physically intimate. But he doesn't pull away, as I half expect him to. His eyes travel down to my lips, the heat in them clear.

He wants this.

Just like I do.

So I close those last few inches between us and kiss him. His lips are just as soft as I remember them being. They move against mine in a clinging, shallow kiss that does more for me than it probably should. It's only a few seconds, but my breath is already coming faster when I pull back, my heart beating fast. I open my mouth to say something, but I don't know what. So I just bite my lip and straighten, taking a step back.

Arawn watches me, the force of his attention strong enough that I feel it on my back when I turn around to go back inside. I move over to my pallet, feeling a little unsteady after only a kiss.

Arawn follows me in a moment later and for a second, I

worry that I gave him the wrong impression, that he thinks I want more than just that kiss.

But I shouldn't have worried. He goes straight to his pallet, settling in with a sigh. Like the gentleman I now know him to be.

"Goodnight, Fallon," he murmurs, his deep voice soothing in the dark.

I swallow, feeling myself relax once more.

"Goodnight, Arawn."

8

ARAWN

J knew our job would be difficult when I agreed to join Errol and Kate. But after several days of talks with the miners, I feel the urge to throw up my hands and leave, allowing Tajss itself to soften them.

"We are a free people who govern ourselves. Why should we accept Rosalind as our tyrant? She has no reason to listen to us. The fact that she keeps sending more Zmaj our way is proof enough that she does not care about our values, the way of life we are trying to create here."

I resist the urge to tell the beady-eyed little man that his values are not worth protecting, even as a small but vocal minority voices their loud agreement with what he just said. He did not have a problem with accepting the supplies we brought.

Jackson raises his hand, though it still takes some time for those people to quiet down. He does not have a very firm hold on the people of the New Village, that much has become abundantly clear the longer we are here and privy to the dynamics of the group.

The fact that most of our talks seem to be public enough

that the New Villagers can come and chime in is not the most helpful setting either. I can see Jackson and this little Elmer male attempting to win those who gather to their side, some of their statements meant more for their people than for us. I cannot help but wonder if at least Jackson would be more amenable without an audience, but we have not had much opportunity to test that theory. When the people finally quiet down, Jackson continues.

"As you can see, we're pretty content governing ourselves," he says, his expression smug as people again voice their agreement. "You may tell Rosalind just that."

I look over at Fallon next to me, but she's having a low conversation with one of the females. I believe her name is Sabrina. Some of the females have warmed up to Fallon and Kate over the last few days, but not all of them. And I do not feel much of that warmth directed towards me or Errol. I wonder how Bashir managed to win them over.

Kate leans forward, her gaze intent. She has obviously had enough as well. Good.

"Look, Jackson. We've been over this again and again—"

A piercing scream interrupts Kate mid-sentence. I am immediately on my feet, lochaber in hand as I look for the threat. Errol steps up to my side as we both look in the direction the scream came from. It was one of sheer terror.

"What was that?" Jackson murmurs, stepping forward slightly more hesitantly. "I have scouts stationed outside the borders of the New Village that should warn us of any danger..." he trails off as we don't hear anything else.

"I think that scream must have been one of those scouts," I point out grimly.

Even as I say it, movement catches our attention.

"Errol."

"Yes," he murmurs. "I see...them."

I can understand his hesitation. What are they?

"Attack! We're under attack!" one of the human males yells in a panic. "Run!"

The humans of the village turn and run in the opposite direction of the unfamiliar group running towards us with intent. But Errol and I step towards them, ready to fight.

"What are those things?" Fallon asks, her tone horrified as she takes them in. "And what do they want?"

"I do not know. Stay back," I order.

Their pole weapons are still in the rover, but because I do not know what these things are or what they can do, I would not want them to engage in any case. Neither Kate nor Fallon argue, but they do not run away as the other humans do.

"Be careful," Fallon calls out as we start to run towards the threat.

"I will," I call back, her concern bolstering me.

Then I put it aside. I need to focus on the attack.

The creatures are not something I have seen before, which leads me to believe they are not native to Tajss. They are not very tall, shorter than the average human male by at least a full head, but their bodies appear quite powerful, the width of their shoulders and the thickness of their arms suggesting strength. They stand on two legs that have joints bending back instead of forward, and their feet appear to be paw-like, though hairless, just like the rest of them.

Textured blue skin covers faces and elongated heads, punctuated by eyes that are full black, no whites or color to them, with thick brow ridges above. The mouths are lipless slits, tusks curving out and around until they almost touch in the front. When one of them yells, the sound is a staccato roar, the opening displaying sharp teeth.

I count six arms in total, three on either side. The arms in the middle are the largest and appear to be the most func-tional, ending in three fingered hands with one joint and black claws at the end. The other four arms are smaller and thinner, ending in what look like small pincers. Everything but the head, hands, and feet appears to be covered by a matte brown carapace-like armor, an emblem of some kind sewn onto the left of the chest. I frown as I see the stylized blue pincer on the brown background. It does not look familiar either. But I do not have time to think on it further.

As we near, I see there is a human male running from the group, having burst out of one of the narrower spaces between buildings, his eyes wide with fear as he runs as quickly as he can.

This is why the human females need the Zmaj to survive here on Tajss. Their males cannot defend even themselves.

We are almost there, but the creatures catch up to the male before we can.

The one nearest makes a powerful leap, latching onto the human's back with all six arms and bringing him down easily, clamping the male's arms to his side with what looks like minimal effort.

Strong.

Another one of the creatures crouches next to the ineffectually struggling male, something small clutched in one of its pincer hands.

Something tipped with a kind of needle. It quickly stabs the struggling human in the neck with the device. Whatever is in that thing it is holding, it works quickly. Judging by the result, it is some kind of drug. Within one breath and the next, the human is completely unconscious.

The thing on his back lets go and pulls out a thin wire from a small pack on its back, obviously with the intent of tying up the now limp human. I notice all this in the short amount of time it takes to close the distance between us and the invaders.

The first one who notices us falters in his forward

momentum, his eyes widening. I smile grimly. They were not expecting to encounter anything but humans here. I am happy to prove them wrong.

I aim directly for the one that hesitates, swinging my lochaber in a hard arc that cuts through air with a low hum, slamming into the thing's side with a crunch. It does not cut through the armor, but the force of the blow is great enough that the protection crumples in, the hit crushing the thing's side.

It immediately drops, clutching at its side while making a high-pitched wheezing sound. I use the opportunity to slit its throat with the sharp blade at the end of my weapon.

I do not wait to watch its death throes, moving on to the next one still tying up the unconscious human. It lets out that staccato yell once more as I kick it in the face.

It ducks down and grabs at my legs with all of its arms. It gets a firm grip, giving me a chance to assess its strength. Very strong. Not unbreakable, but I might struggle against it in the right circumstances.

Fortunately, it makes the mistake of forgetting my arms as it yanks me down to the ground. I flip my lochaber and stab down with the blunt end, aiming for its eye. I break through the skull with a crack. The thing goes limp, still wrapped around me.

I shake free and leap back to my feet, ready to take on more attackers, but I only see their backs now as the remainder flee, their unusual legs helping them bound away quickly.

When I look over at Errol, I see him drop one of the creatures to the ground, its limp body giving the news that it is no longer a threat. His eyes are also on the fast-retreating figures.

"Should we pursue?" I wonder out loud.

Errol hesitates, but Fallon cuts in, closer than I would like. How near did she get during the fight?

"No," she says. "What if they circle back around while you guys are gone? Or if there are more of them waiting to come in from another direction? The whole village will be sitting ducks just waiting for the slaughter."

"Fallon is right," Kate agrees. "Better to stay."

Errol and I both nod. The reasoning is sound. When we turn back around to see how the humans are faring, it is to see an empty square behind us. I blink at it.

"They closed themselves off inside," Fallon observes, her tone a touch scathing. "Never mind the fact that there are broken windows and doors and literal holes in some of the walls."

"They'd be better off forming a circle with weapons, protecting each other's backs," Kate agrees, shaking her head.

Our voices must alert them to the fact that it is safe enough to come back out from hiding, because doors start to open slowly, heads peeking out to cast wary glances at the now empty square. Well, empty except for us, the dead invaders, and the one still unconscious human.

Jackson comes out before the others, looking down at the ground grimly.

"It's safe everyone," he calls out, attempting to take charge once more, though he just ran from the danger as did everyone else. Not that he would have been a help. I doubt he would have been able to do much more than be attacked, like his fellow villager.

But the first thing he does when he comes out is go over to the still unconscious male, a decision that makes me think better of him.

"Tessa, can you help me untie him?" he asks.

The brunette hurries over to him, getting to work quickly. In short order, the man is carried away, still unconscious. I hope there are no lasting effects. Considering they were attempting to kidnap him and not kill him, I think he will most likely be fine.

"What about the bodies?" Jackson mutters to himself as people start to gather enough courage to step up to them.

I see a few nudge the bodies with their feet, ensuring they are actually gone and not a threat.

"I would suggest taking them far from the village borders in order to avoid drawing unwanted attention from those who would want the meat," Errol says.

Gruesome, but sound advice. Jackson grimaces and nods.

"But what the hell are these things?" he asks, shaking his head as he stares down at the bodies. "I haven't seen anything like them while here on Tajss. They're obviously intelligent."

"I do not know," Errol admits. "Arawn?"

I shake my head.

"They are not native to Tajss. But beyond that..." I do not have any more information than that.

Errol nods, frowning.

"There is something about that symbol, something almost familiar." He shakes his head. "All I can say is, judging from the fact that they did not kill that male, it appears as though they were here to kidnap you."

That sends a wave of unease through the group of those listening, with good reason. Jackson's jaw tightens, but he cannot deny the truth of that. Or the fact that they would have had no defense against the attack had we not been here to fight for them.

"Send someone to go check on the scouts," Jackson tells Tessa. Then he turns to us. "Follow me please."

We all look at each other, but then follow a step behind Jackson. He takes us away from the square, away from the crowd. Most of it is still distracted by the shock of what just occurred, but I see many noting our departure. When we appear to be at a safe enough distance to have some privacy, Jackson begins to speak.

"It is quite clear to me that we were lucky you were here just now," he starts abruptly, not happy about that fact. But willing to acknowledge it. It is a start.

"They only ran because of Errol and Arawn," Kate agrees.

Jackson nods.

"Yes." He continues to lead us away. "You might think we are stupid to refuse to be brought under Rosalind's thumb despite the fact that we plainly need aid." He glances over at us, smiling thinly when none of us deny his assertion. "I would argue we aren't stupid, just careful. Yes, our lives aren't easy right now, but we're in control of them. And we want to keep it that way."

"But?" Fallon prods.

Jackson sends her a look that is not very friendly, but he lets out a breathy sigh directly after, looking away.

"But. This is not the first time the Zmaj have saved us from a threat." He nods at me and then at Errol. "Thank you on behalf of the New Village."

Errol and I acknowledge the thanks with nods of our own.

"That brings me back to my initial point," he continues, stopping in front of a dark, stone-lined entrance. Obviously, the entrance to the mines, or at least one of them. "We are not stupid. And this attack...changes things."

"You are willing to ally with Rosalind and the Tribe?" Errol asks.

Jackson tilts his head, wincing at the question.

"Ally is a strong word. I would like to discuss an... arrangement. A trade arrangement. Where we receive protection in exchange for some of the ore we have." He gestures to the entrance. "To show I make the offer in good faith, I have brought you to the mine myself."

Errol and I exchange a look. Metal is rare on Tajss now, and therefore more valuable. Currently, the mines the New Village control are the only source of it apart from scavenging for it. The trade is not a bad one.

"We can't agree to a trade like that without input from Rosalind," Kate says carefully, watching Jackson. "But allowing us see the ore you've found is a good first step. We'll be sure to pass on the fact that you were so cooperative when we see Rosalind."

He looks around at us.

"I can take one of you inside to show you what we have uncovered so far. The way is often narrow and I'm not that confident about how stable everything is down there."

Perhaps.

Or perhaps he does not want so many of us to have ready knowledge of the layout of the mines.

"I can go," I offer, looking at the others. "I am familiar with many of the metals that could be found here."

Errol and Kate agree.

"Be careful," Fallon urges. "And don't stay down there too long."

"I will take care," I reassure her, smiling at her softly.

If we were alone, I would kiss her as softly as she kissed me last night. I have been thinking of that kiss all day. But I do not yet know what boundaries she desires, how much she is willing to share with others. So I resist and instead simply follow Jackson into the mines.

He leads me through a circuitous route, one that would have taken me much longer to find on my own. And what I see is enough to determine that they do indeed have a good amount of bargaining power. The glimmer and shimmer of the varieties of ore he shows me by torchlight are valuable.

Very valuable.

I can already think of many uses they could be put to,

both in the city's technology and for everyday use in weapons, utensils, and so many more items.

"We've been digging through to see how deep the veins go," Jackson informs me, gesturing to where the work has obviously been focused. "We haven't found the end yet. And there's still more of the mine that we haven't gone through yet, but I've shown you where we think a lot of the usable and readily available ore is located."

"I think I have seen enough."

"I just hope I made the right decision," he says in a low voice, staring at what they have uncovered.

"I think you have made the only rational one." I fully believe that to be the case.

"Yes," he murmurs.

With nothing else to say, he leads me back out of the narrow tunnels, back to where the others wait for us.

I see the relief wash over Fallon's face when I reappear and have to resist the urge to make physical contact again. I bite back a growl. The restraint I must show is frustrating to say the least. I want more, now. But I cannot rush things and risk ruining the progress we have made. So I do not act on what I feel.

By the time we make it back to the village, it is time for the communal meal once more. The bodies have been taken away quite efficiently, though marks of the purplish blood remain on the ground to clean up later. The food is being served in a different area today, one where we do not need to eat near the area where the attack actually occurred. I appreciate whoever decided on the change.

Our small group sits down at a table with our plates and I start to eat, hungry from the full day.

But no sooner has everyone gathered that trouble begins to brew once more. It begins with someone sitting near that same balding, beady-eyed man who seems to always be working against Jackson. The man who stands is thin, with fine, light colored hair.

"Jackson, how could you betray us like you did?" he cries out, looking around to ensure he has everyone's attention. His dramatic opening ensures that he does. "How could you take these people to the mines, to the very source of any power that we have?"

A beat of silence at that accusation.

Jackson's face turns red and I see him begin to rise from his chair. But others jump into the fight before he does.

"We need the Zmaj, you idiot!" Sabrina calls out. "Look at what we did when we were attacked! We ran!"

"Not to mention the fact that they brought us food! What have you brought us?" someone else chimes in.

"Yeah, I'm tired of the bullshit—we need help and I'm not ashamed to admit it!"

The crowd breaks into pandemonium, with people trying to shout over each other, though it is clear the majority are leaning more towards Rosalind, more towards accepting our help. Those that are still willing to hold onto their human stubbornness past the point of reason are a much smaller number.

Finally, some progress.

Jackson stands, shouting to be heard above the level of noise generated by the crowd.

"This discussion is no longer a reasonable one to have!" he shouts, the last of those still speaking slowly quieting. "Would those of you opposed to dealing with Rosalind and the Zmaj rather starve? Or die in a gruesome manner when the next threat arrives, and we are unprepared?" He shakes his head as he gives Elmer a look. "We have been taking their food and making use of their protection as though it could not be taken away tomorrow. We need something more stable, something we can count on. And I am not willing to die because of our unwillingness to adapt, to change as need- ed." There are still grumbles from the crowd, but they subside as Jackson introduces a new subject. "Now, these attackers. You don't recognize them?" he asks, directing the question at us once more.

"No," I say shaking my head.

"The symbols they wore are familiar," Errol says once more, his eyes distant. A moment where he strains to reach for the memory. But he ultimately shakes his head in defeat when it does not come. "It must be something from long ago. I cannot remember exactly why it is familiar. However, I do not need to know where the symbol is from to reasonably assume they were here to kidnap people. It is what the Zzlo are famous for and the fact that these invaders did not kill anyone points to the same conclusion."

"Kidnapping." Jackson shakes his head, clearly disturbed. "Could they come back?" he prods.

Errol nods.

"Yes. They obviously know you are here. That is why they attacked."

"So we are vulnerable, even more so than before," Jackson announces, ensuring everyone can hear him. It is clear he is justifying what he is going to say next when he says it. "That is why I would like to send someone to the city to discuss a trade arrangement. One where we trade Zmaj protection for ore, firmly establishing several of the Zmaj here in the mining settlement."

Even before the outcry begins, I know there will be one. Jackson is taking a risk, even though the majority are clearly with him. On the other hand, not doing something could mean that all of these people might not be around to lead in any case. It is a difficult position to be in, but he decided he wanted it.

As predicted, people start trying to shout him down

again. But they quiet down when Elmer gestures to them, turning their shouts to murderous glares instead.

Trouble.

But we have sensed that since we arrived. That man has too much power among those that follow him.

Errol leans over to whisper to me.

"We need to travel back to the city and the Tribe's caves to report this development. If there are even more creatures out there looking to kidnap..."

I nod. We need to warn everyone. Protecting ourselves against beasts is one thing. Their behavior can be predicted, their methods outsmarted. But an intelligent threat is something we will need to take even more precautions for. And we need to report the New Villagers' softening of opinion to Rosalind as well.

I doubt those beings will attack the New Village so quickly after this first failed attempt, but the longer we wait before we leave, the higher the chances are that they might regroup and return. These people need protection as soon as possible.

All in all, this visit has not gone at all like I thought it might.

9

FALLON

*A*fter the day we had, I really need a bath. Luckily, that's something I can actually have. I sigh as I lay my head back in the giant bathtub we found in one of the other rooms. Arawn was nice enough to help me carry enough water inside to fill it up just enough to be useful.

I really miss indoor plumbing, but at least it's always so hot here that I don't even worry about the water not being warm enough. Tepid or even cool feels amazing after sweating all day.

I loll around in the water longer than I need to, but what else am I going to do at this time of day anyway? So I stubbornly stay in long after my fingertips are wrinkly and call it time well spent. Still, I can't just become a fish. So I eventually I call it and get out of the tub, reaching for one of the drying cloths we brought with us.

I'm glad we packed for staying out in the desert because the New Villagers really haven't done much to accommodate us. Though after Errol and Arawn protected them so fiercely from those weird looking aliens, they're obviously thinking twice about being so unwelcoming.

There's definitely been a softening towards our group, especially towards the Zmaj. A noticeable one. It's kind of irritating to realize it's because these people see that Arawn and Errol are useful, but maybe the reasoning shouldn't matter so much as long as we get what we set out for here.

It's difficult to divorce my feelings from it though. I feel protective of Arawn now. I don't like the idea of people thinking of him only as a useful commodity rather than a person. But I can't control everyone's thoughts. That's a losing battle.

I briskly rub myself dry, hearing my stomach growl a complaint. I need to go forage for some food. I wrap the cloth around me and tuck it in at my chest to keep it in place before I move back out into the room where we have our pallets.

I hesitate as I see the cloth Arawn has spread over the floor, food laid out on it picnic style, that same fat candle lit, casting a warm glow.

"You already prepared dinner for us?" I ask, feeling a rush of warmth. At the same time, I make sure the drying cloth is tucked tightly around me.

He nods, his eyes heating as he takes in my bare arms and legs, the top of my chest. But he looks away, ever the gentleman. Sweet.

"Please, sit."

He gestures to the small cushions he's fashioned with blankets. I sink down onto one, sitting on my calves and keeping my legs together. I feel even more vulnerable without all my clothes on, but maybe I could just eat quickly and then grab them.

"Thank you, Arawn," I murmur as he hands me a plate. "I'm really hungry."

He smiles.

"Of course. I knew we both would be."

I smile back at him, taking a bite of the food. There's a zing of tension in the air, but it isn't the awkward kind as we sit and eat, talking about both the invaders and the reaction of the New Villagers. It's more like we're both just very aware of the other. At least, I know I am.

"At least they have come to their senses and most are acknowledging they need Zmaj help," he muses.

"It's only their racism that has kept them from admitting it for so long." I shake my head. How they thought they could afford the luxury of such irrational thoughts is beyond me. I couldn't even imagine refusing Gomul's help when he arrived to save us.

"Hmm." He reaches back to pull out a small bundle. "I have a gift for you as well, Fallon."

"A gift?" I ask, staring at the small package. "You didn't have to, Arawn," I protest even as he hands it to me. "You've done enough."

He shakes his head.

"I wanted to. Please, open it," he urges eagerly.

I smile, taken by his unhidden eagerness. It's so sweet. And isn't it telling that I keep describing him that way? I unwrap the small piece of leather it's wrapped in, curious as to what could be inside...

"A book!" I exclaim, staring down at the well-worn cover, excitement rushing through me as I trace the title. "*The Lord of the Rings*!"

"I understand it is a popular story," Arawn comments. "I bargained for it with some of the meteorite glass jewelry Errol has me trading with the miners." A pause. "Do you like it?"

I nod vigorously, clutching the book in my hands as I look back up at him.

"I love it," I say sincerely. "It's a treasure. I know I'll read it over and over again." I hug it to my chest. "I'm so glad some of the old things survived the crash," I add, feeling misty eyed at the thought of how much didn't.

It isn't an exaggeration to call this a treasure. Not when so many of our books, our movies, everything our society created is lost forever.

In my excitement, I must have pressed the book too hard into myself because I feel the cloth wrapped around me start to slip. I grab at it quickly, holding it up with my free hand as a blush heats my face.

"Oops," I mutter. "Probably I should dress."

Arawn's eyes are locked on my hand, the only thing keeping me somewhat covered. The fire in his expression is hot enough to heat the room.

I feel a heat of a different kind flow through me at that look.

But he doesn't act on it. Nodding, he stands.

I feel a sharp stab of disappointment.

"I will wait outside," he offers, turning to the door.

I bite my lip as he takes a step towards it and realize I don't want him to go.

"Wait," I call out, setting the book down and scrambling to my feet.

He turns around, a question on his face.

This is it. I can't use alcohol as an excuse if I do this. Not this time. My mind is as clear as it gets. My choices completely my own. I meet Arawn's eyes and make the decision.

I open my hand.

The cloth drops to my feet.

Leaving me naked. Completely bare in more ways than just the physical. Completely vulnerable.

"Fallon," he murmurs, his cheeks flushed as his eyes leave my face. I see his hands clench into fists at his side, his tail twitch behind him. "Are you certain?"

I feel tenderness mix with the heat, the fire that's been building between us. This is more than physical now, more than that attraction I've felt from the beginning. I know him as a person, know how brave he is, how giving, how considerate.

I know Arawn. I want him. All of him.

Who knows what tomorrow will bring? What I've learned not just on this trip, but in my time here on Tajss so far, is that there's always a threat looming just on the horizon. Tomorrow is no guarantee. I don't want to regret not living life to its fullest just because I was afraid. So here we are.

Time to seize the fucking day.

"Yes. I'm as sure as I've ever been of anything."

That's the green light he needed, the last push to break free. With a growl, he closes the distance between us in two long strides, his arms coming up to wrap around me. He pulls me to him firmly, his lips coming down to meet mine, hard and voracious. It isn't pretty or soft. And it's exactly what I want.

I rise up on my toes in an attempt to get closer, my hands sliding over his shoulders, sinking into his silky hair. He hooks an arm under my leg, raising it to wrap around his hip.

I feel exactly how aroused he is as he pushes against me, rubs his hard cock against my core. Where I'm aching and ready for him. All of him.

Abruptly, he picks me up and pushes me against the wall, raising me so the difference in our heights doesn't get in the way.

His hand slides up my side to close over my breast. He groans as he kneads it, breaking the kiss.

"You are so soft. Everywhere," he says hoarsely, resting his forehead against my own as he angles his head down to look at what he's doing. He rubs at my nipple experimentally. I arch against him at the sharp sensation. "Does that feel good?" he asks, repeating the stroke with his thumb.

"Yes," I gasp. "It's good. Did Zmaj women not have breasts?" I ask, wondering at his curiosity.

"They were protected by scales, opening for feeding only. Not for males, not for pleasure," he explains.

And then he doesn't want to talk anymore. Which is perfectly fine with me.

Lifting me up higher, he latches onto my nipple with a hard suck that has my toes curling in response, my head kicking back against the wall. I barely feel my head hit the hard surface, but Arawn immediately lifts me away, turning with me and taking us down onto my pallet, which is closer.

Then he gets up again and rips off his clothes, his glittering eyes locked on me as he does. I feel an edge in the look, feeling almost like prey. But it only ratchets my arousal up higher.

When he comes back down on top of me, both of us moan as skin only meets skin now. I run my fingers up his back and then lightly over the tops of his wings.

He gasps, leaning down to kiss me again, his tongue tangling with mine as his hands run over my body desperately. Just as mine do over his.

He uses his legs to push mine apart, settling between them as his hand slides down my stomach, zeroing in on where I ache for him. I jerk as his fingers slide through my wet folds once before stopping at my clitoris.

He breaks the kiss, his eyes focusing on my no-doubt glazed ones as he rubs and pinches at it softly.

"I know this part gives you pleasure," he murmurs, circling with the tips of his fingers.

I nod, swallowing as I try to focus.

"Yes. That's my...clitoris," I gasp as he gives it a harder pinch, obviously testing how I respond.

"Too much?" he asks.

I shake my head no.

"It feels...good." Really good.

He takes me at my word, rubbing and exploring, alternating between burying his face against my breasts and kissing me as I feel myself getting closer and closer to that final destination.

"I must taste you," he growls, sliding down to settle between my legs. Even just the words drive me closer.

I look down just as his tongue comes out to lick at me.

That's it.

Too much.

I cry out, bucking against his mouth as I come, the wave of pleasure almost painful. He keeps his mouth on me until I come back down, his tongue soft and comforting against me.

I'm panting, trying to catch my breath as he comes back up, kissing me softly. I can taste myself on his lips. And I can feel another part of him nudging at me.

"Fallon?" he asks, kissing the side of my face, my neck, as he rubs against me.

"Come inside me," I urge, reaching down to grip his hard ass cheeks.

He groans, kissing me deeply at that request, and then he starts to push in.

I take a deep breath, breaking the kiss to look down. I have a vague memory of the ridges that run along the top of his cock, but seeing it again—it's pretty eye-catching.

I bite my lip as his impressive size stretches me, those ridges at the top bumping against my clit just right as he slowly, carefully, slides in.

I shut my eyes tight when he's finally in all the way, the ridge at the very base of him pressing up against me...so...good.

And then he starts to move. I grip his arms, my fingernails digging into his hard muscle as he pushes in and out of me. It's almost too much. Almost.

Bracing himself on his forearms, his eyes are locked with mine as he continues to thrust, his big, muscled body moving like a well-oiled machine.

I feel completely dominated and more feminine that I've ever felt in my life, covered and surrounded by Arawn. But I also know he'll keep me safe, and that he would never hurt me.

I thrust back up against him experimentally and he lets out a harsh sound. So I do it again. And again. Until I'm making small sounds in the back of my throat, and his jaw is clenched hard enough that the cords stand out in high relief.

This time, we get there together.

I force myself to keep my eyes open as his shut, his entire body straining as I feel him jerk inside me, his thrusts no longer smooth and coordinated.

The connection between us is so deep, I feel like I can almost feel...him. Not just his body, but the spiritual force that is the essence of him. Like we're absorbing parts of each other that aren't just physical. In that moment, that idea doesn't sound silly at all. It sounds completely possible.

When he opens his eyes again, they're slumberous with pleasure, but still hot. He pulls out of me, slowly, making my entire body arch as all the sensitized nerve endings are hit once more.

Then he reaches down, adjusting his second cock. I swallow hard, staring down at it. I heard the Zmaj men have two penises, the second one tucked under the tail. But again, hearing and seeing are two completely different ballgames. He rolls me gently onto my side and draws my leg over his hip, taking me from behind now.

This time is much gentler, his movements careful, cognizant of the fact that I'm already sensitive. He kisses my ear, the back of my neck, the arm tucked under me curving up to cup one breast. While the other reaches between my legs, his fingers getting involved. When I get there this time, the orgasm is also softer, a warm wave that has me sighing, pressing back against him. He buries his face in the curve of my shoulder, his own climax shuddering through him right after mine.

We stay like that, with him wrapped around me, as our breathing calms down, our pulse rates return back to normal. His arm wraps around my waist, hugging me back to him tightly, his body cupping the back of mine in a warm line.

"Fallon...I could not have imagined you to be any more extraordinary than I had previously thought, but after tonight..."

I chuckle, shaking my head as I turn slightly and reach up to cup the side of his sweet face.

"That's just the sex talking, Arawn."

He kisses my palm but shakes his head.

"No, it is not. I felt...I experienced the depth of your life force." He looks at me intently. "You are strong. Very strong. There is far more to you than anyone realizes. Than I realized."

I would dismiss what he's saying as emotional pillow talk, but it sounds so similar to what I thought I felt. Maybe it was real.

I feel the afterglow give way to another kind of warmth, one perhaps even more important. The fact that he recognizes my strength, the very part of me that my father tried to suppress from the moment I was old enough to take orders from him...it means so much. He doesn't want to suppress it. He admires it.

I can almost feel my heart opening up to Arawn as I look

into his gorgeous eyes. It's a feeling I know I cannot ignore. And, frankly, I don't want to avoid it. Not anymore.

I raise a brow as I feel something else stir inside me. Something more tangible.

"Again?" I ask, incredulous.

Arawn grins, even as he shifts to thrust inside me, where he never left.

"Fallon, I have been starving for you," he admits, his smile fading. "It will take me a long time to sate myself."

Well then. I sigh as his hands start to move on me with purpose again. I'm willing to make the sacrifice for his wellbeing.

Poor me.

10

ARAWN

$\mathcal{W}$e leave for the city the next morning. We have to take the news of the invaders back to Rosalind and the others, along with the New Villagers' softening stance over some kind of alliance or at least trade agreement. There is no time to waste.

As we pack up the rover, Jackson and a few villagers gather to make their farewells. Saying our send-off from the New Village is warm would be overstating matters, but it is undoubtedly warmer than the reception we received on our arrival.

"Let Rosalind know we would like to expedite the process of the exchange," Jackson says as we stand ready to climb into the vehicle. "I do not want to wait so long that the point might become moot," he says grimly.

We all know what he means by that.

"We will," Kate reassures him. "If she agrees to the trade— and I have a feeling she will—you won't be out here alone for long."

He nods, stepping back.

"Have a safe journey."

"Thank you."

We all wave goodbye to those who have gathered to see us off and then climb into the rover, ready to leave.

"Let's hit the road," Kate mutters, starting it up and turning it in a wide circle.

Within moments, we are already a good distance away from the village and all of the politics we had to deal with for days. I feel my shoulders relax for the first time since we arrived at the mining settlement.

"Man, I'm really glad to be out of there," Fallon announces, sighing. "It was so tiring to always be watching what I was saying, keeping an eye over my shoulder in case someone decided getting rid of us was a good idea."

"I hear you," Kate agrees. "And if one more person glared at me when I touched Errol...let's just say I'm glad we're out of there," she finishes, reaching out to pat Errol's thigh.

He covers Kate's hand with his own.

"Agreed."

"Yes. It was not an easy trip," I add.

The mood is one of recovery. We accomplished what we set out to do. Now we can relax somewhat. We travel for hours, stopping only for necessary breaks. None of us want the trip to be longer than necessary. But, eventually, the suns start their downward trajectory once more.

"I think we can travel for another hour before we must stop for the night," Errol observes. "Unless there is some good shelter nearby?"

"I can go do a quick scout," I offer. "I believe there might be some rock formations in this direction."

"I can come with you," Fallon chimes in immediately. "I want to stretch my legs too after sitting for so long."

Errol and Kate exchange a knowing glance. I do not mind. I want everyone to know we are together.

"All right," Kate says easily. "Don't go too far—we should

get a move on to find another location if there's nothing good nearby."

"We will be quick," I reassure her.

Fallon follows me over the dune I gestured at. We are out of sight of the others and the rover almost immediately, but I automatically keep track of our direction and distance. It is a simple matter to lose oneself in the desert. Being aware of that fact is a kind of protection in and of itself.

"How far are these rock formations?" Fallon asks as she walks along beside me. "Maybe it would be better if—"

Something slams into the sand in front of us, hard and fast, sending a pelting spray up. My hearts immediately start racing.

Meteorites.

They are an all-too-familiar phenomenon now. I look up, seeing the grouping of burning rocks blackening the sky above us.

"Arawn!" Fallon cries out, ducking as another one hits the sand nearby.

There is no time to plan.

Fallon is within arm's length, so I reach out and pull her to me, picking up her negligible weight. Flaring my wings out to protect her from the rocks falling all around us, I start to run in the direction I think the shelter is—and hope my memory has not failed me.

A rock hits the shield of my wings, the searing pain of the flame and the impact making me wince even as I continue to run.

"Arawn! Your wings!" Fallon gasps. "They're getting burned!"

She shifts in my arms as if to leave them, but I tighten my hold on her.

"I will be fine," I reassure her, pushing the pain back as

another rock batters my wings. "Do not struggle—I will be hurt far worse if you are hurt."

She stills, her body trembling slightly in my arms, but she does not struggle again.

I run as fast as I can, unable to properly use my wings to propel us forward because I need them spread to protect Fallon. But I travel quickly even so.

"There!" Fallon cries out over the sound of the rocks hitting the ground. "Rocks!"

I turn in the direction she is pointing, so focused on speed that I didn't at first notice the rocks. I put on another burst of speed, the burning in my wings growing worse. The pain is bad, but I am more worried that my wings will crumple under the onslaught, leaving Fallon vulnerable. That is unacceptable.

"Hold on tightly," I order, adjusting my hold on her so I can lengthen my stride.

As we draw closer, I see an area where there appears to be a series of caverns in the large rock formation, most of them appearing shallow. One looks as though it is quite deep.

I aim for that one with that last burst of speed. I stumble in, catching my balance quickly, grimacing as I gingerly put Fallon down.

Fallon hisses as she steps around me to look at my wings.

"I wish we had something to put on them," she murmurs, touching the edge of one wing. "I don't like that we're separated from Kate and Errol either. Maybe one of them would know what to do." A flash of concern crosses her face. "I hope they're okay."

I take a deep breath, happy that she is now out of danger. I look around the cavern. It looks somewhat familiar, though the memory is old. Very old.

"Do not worry—I know Errol would have gotten Kate to safety, likely using the rover. We will find them again after the storm passes." I glance around once more, hazy memory resurfacing. "And I believe there might be a spring deeper in this cavern," I say out loud.

Perhaps my memories aimed me here for that reason.

"Water?" Fallon asks, perking up. "That's exactly what we need for your wings. Come on!"

Taking my hand in hers, she starts tugging me deeper into the cave. I allow her to do so, my eyes sharp as I watch where she is putting her feet and what is directly ahead of us. It is not unheard of to find creatures lurking in natural shelters just like this one. Sometimes dangerous ones.

We hear a small skittering at one point, but it is clearly a small creature. Fallon jumps at the sound all the same.

"It is no danger to us," I reassure her. "And I believe the spring is just ahead," I add to distract her.

I am right about the spring.

We turn around a natural bend, the smell of fresh water permeating this short corridor, and the sound of its trickling echoing before reaching our ears. Fallon speeds up.

The end of the narrower tunnel opens up into a much larger cavern room. Light streams in from narrow cracks above, though none of them are very wide, making it safe even in the meteorite shower.

In the center of the cave, there is a wide spring, filled with fresh water filtered through the rock, clear and clean.

Along the edges, taking advantage of the water source and the light streaming in, are small bushes growing nefetter fruit. Shaped like two connected globes and red in color when ripe, the fruit is known for both its sweetness and its filling quality.

"Oh, wow. This place is gorgeous," Fallon says, her eyes wide as they look around.

"Yes," I agree. "And we can eat the fruit as well."

"Really?" she glances at the fruit, considering, but then

shakes her head. "First, we need to see to your wings. Come on—you have to undress."

I do not argue as she helps me take my clothes off. Not when she takes hers off directly after to join me in the water.

"Perhaps I should find myself in a meteorite shower more often," I tease as she carefully cups water and lets it run over my wings, the cooling sensation very welcome. As is the sight of her bared breasts swaying with her movements. Unable to resist, I reach out to cup the soft curves, enamored with them since I first saw them. Fallon stills, blushing as she meets my eyes.

"You're hurt," she murmurs.

"I am not that hurt," I counter, drawing her into my arms. "My wings feel better. Thank you."

She settles her hands on my chest.

"I still don't think it's a good idea to..."

She trails off with a sigh as I lift her to my mouth, settling the matter with a kiss. I can still feel my hearts beating faster than normal from being caught outside in the meteorite shower. And the thrill of being alive. I cannot think of a better way to celebrate than with my mate.

Mate.

It could not be clearer that Fallon is exactly that to me.

My mate.

The realization settles into me with a sense of rightness as I urge her to wrap her legs around my waist, my mouth still playing over hers. The warmth that meets my cock, the wetness signaling her readiness, make me groan. I push in gently, but firmly, using small strokes to make room for myself in her. I have to be patient. She is so small, so delicate.

She breaks the kiss, crying out, "Arawn!"

Her fingers dig into my shoulders as I push in to the hilt. I grit my teeth as I feel the tight clasp of her over my entire length. Gripping her hips in my hands, I lift her up off my cock. And then back down. She gasps, and I groan.

I can go even deeper into her at this angle. The coupling is deep and slow. I force myself to rein in my thrusts, wanting it to last. Fallon's eyes are closed, her cheeks flushed, her teeth biting into her soft bottom lip as she makes small mewling cries that have my cock jerking inside her. I do not last long despite my effort at restraint.

Reaching between us, I rub at her small nub as I feel my orgasm begin, not wanting to leave her behind. She cries out, bucking against me, clenching down on me hard. I shudder, pulling her down on me all the way, seating myself deeply. The pleasure is so great I have to spread my legs, brace myself so I do not tumble us both into the water.

It takes some time for me to catch my breath, for my muscles to stop their trembling. Once I am steady, I wade in deeper with Fallon still in my arms, allowing the spring to wash us, to soothe my wings. We drift in the water for a few moments, enjoying the sensation, but then Fallon's belly growls with hunger.

"I will go get the fruit," I say, kissing her forehead.

So we climb out and Fallon sits along the edge of the water as I go to the wall of the cavern. The bushes grow along the wall near the water, turning to vines halfway up. The ripe fruit is on those vines, the fruit more easily accessible still green.

Spreading my wings, I leap up to reach the edible fruit and start gathering it, feeling my wings spasm with the effort. But the pain has subsided to a dull ache rather than the searing pain of earlier.

Fallon helps me carry the fruit back to where I first left her.

"You shouldn't have done so much with your wings," she admonishes. "Don't hurt yourself more if you don't have to."

Her concern is only because she cares, and I savor the evidence of that.

"I am fine," I reassure her as I peel one of the fruits. "Here —taste this. I know you will find it delicious."

She takes the peeled, pale pink fruit, letting out a squeak of surprise as it almost slips out of her hands.

"Careful," I warn as I start to peel another, chuckling a bit.

She nods, cupping it carefully as she takes a tentative bite of the nefetter. Her eyes widen.

"Oh, this is really good!" she exclaims, taking a bigger bite.

I grin, pleased at her pleasure.

"Yes. We are quite lucky to have found so much of it here."

She nods enthusiastically.

"I would never have been able to reach the fruit that high up," she says, glancing along the wall. "Thank you, Arawn." She looks at me seriously, reaching out to cover my hand with her own. "For the fruit, for saving me. Again."

I shake my head, handing her more fruit and squeezing her hand.

"I will always put your life before mine, Fallon."

She searches my eyes, nodding.

"I would do the same for you," she murmurs. "I've never felt this way about anyone. Not even my father," she adds with a trembling smile

I know she tells the truth. I raise her hand and kiss it softly.

"Then I know you have given me a true treasure," I say, holding her hand tightly.

She tells me more as we eat the sweet fruit. About life on the ship. About her relationship with her father. About her mother and how she abdicated all responsibility after she gave birth.

"Sorry," Fallon says, chuckling as she looks away, though

it is without humor. "I don't know why I'm dumping all of this on you."

"I want to hear it," I reassure her. "I want to know everything about you."

She meets my eyes again.

"Well, you now officially know more than anyone else," she tells me with a trembling smile.

I pull her into a tight hug, wanting to take all of her pain. Knowing it is part of what formed her, part of what created the wonderful person she is today. I feel us grow even closer that night, as we lie down together to wait until the meteorite storm has passed. I tell her about myself, about my first hunt. About my family.

I feel every word we say binding us closer, small threads that combine to make a sturdy rope.

11

FALLON

*T*he night I spend with Arawn is...unforgettable. Again, he's managed to save us, but it's more than that. It's what it signifies, what it means. He cares. Really cares about me.

The fact that he would sustain those burns to shield me from the meteor shower, not even taking his own safety into account, prioritizing me before himself... I've never felt so loved, so important to someone. Words can be cheap, but I can't argue against actions.

What started as a harrowing ordeal changed into a secluded retreat for the two of us that I could never have predicted. One that I'm almost sad to see is over when dawn's light starts to creep into the cavern. Go figure.

Arawn rises early and collects some more fruit for us, his powerful legs flexing as he leaps up, his back muscles standing out beautifully as he spreads his wings to help him reach higher. I'm glad to see his wings are mostly healed already, the angry-looking burns greatly faded. I've never been happier about the Zmaj's robust physicality, their rapid ability to heal.

But that's definitely not all I'm noticing. I ogle him unashamedly. He's simply gorgeous. And naked. Deliciously naked. When he turns around with fruit in hand, I give the front of him the same amount of attention. He smiles at me as he walks over and sits down to start peeling the fruit.

"Is something amiss?" he asks, handing a peeled fruit to me first.

I shake my head, taking it.

"No. You're just really nice to look at."

His smile widens.

"I am glad you think so." His eyes scan my own naked form. "But I must say, you are much better to look at than I am."

I laugh, shaking my head.

"I think this definitely falls into 'whatever floats your boat' territory."

He cocks his head to the side in question.

"'Floats your boat'?" he asks, taking a bite of his own fruit.

"Whatever you yourself like," I explain.

His face clears as he chews.

"Ah. Perhaps." He glances towards the bend that leads outside, quickly finishing the filling fruit. "I will go see if the meteorites have ceased falling. We need to leave if they have."

I nod, watching as he dresses quickly and leaves to investigate.

We still have some distance to travel. I really hope Errol and Kate are okay. Those meteorite showers are no joke. They could seriously injure or even kill if they hit properly. But, as Arawn said, they had the rover to take shelter in and perhaps find somewhere to spend the night. And they're both capable people.

Arawn is back within a few minutes, which is good. I could feel my worry about the rest of group starting to spiral.

"It is safe to leave," he says, reaching down to help me to my feet.

I nod. I guess our little escape from reality is over. I grab my clothes and dress quickly as well. With nothing to pack apart from some more pieces of fruit, we're ready to leave the cavern in less than five minutes.

I blink at the light as we step outside, the early morning light still soft as it casts a pink glow over the red sand, but much brighter than the dimness inside.

Squinting, I realize part of the brightness is due to the way it glimmers off the glass where the meteorites melted the sand, the heat of the fire changing the structure of it.

The scene looks spectacular. A glittering landscape that looks both alien and whimsical. Sometimes I forget that Tajss has its own particular kind of harsh beauty. Usually, I'm too worried about the heat and possible threats to truly appreciate it.

"Where do you think we should go?" I ask as we take a moment to absorb the vista we find. I find myself speaking in an unnecessarily hushed tone.

"The first place we should check is where we last saw Errol and Kate. It is likely where Errol will go as well if they are able."

That makes sense. So we travel the distance back with Arawn's arm wrapped around me to help me traverse the sand faster. The journey back seems quite a bit longer now that we aren't running for our lives. Imagine that.

"The location is just past this next dune," Arawn says.

I nod, mentally crossing my fingers. Please be there...

Luckily, we crest the rise, and there they are.

Errol and Kate stand leaning against the rover, looking whole and uninjured. Even the rover doesn't look much worse for wear. They straighten when they see us, the wash of relief over the faces mirroring how we feel to find them safe and in one piece. They meet us halfway as we descend, hurrying over as soon as they spot us.

I hug Kate back as she rushes forward to pull me into her.

"Oh my God, I'm so glad you guys are all right!" she cries out, letting go of me to look over at Errol as well. "We at least had the rover, but you guys were completely vulnerable!"

Arawn nods.

"We were able to find a cavern to take shelter in," he explains. He holds out the fruit. "And we found nefetter there as well."

"Arawn found the cavern," I clarify. "And lucky he did. I don't know how long we would have lasted out there in that storm."

Kate nods, her face turning serious.

"Yeah. We hopped into the rover and found a ridge with some overhang to hunker down in. It's lucky that you found something so close."

"Very true."

I notice something else that catches my eye.

Errol has a bag of something in hand, a bag that looks quite full.

"What's that?" I ask curiously, gesturing at it. "Did you find something else?"

Errol opens up the bag to show us the contents.

"It is meteorite glass," he explains, the sparkling contents giving it away even before he names it. "I just have a... feeling," he murmurs, frowning down at it, his expression turning distant as he stares.

"What kind of feeling?" Arawn asks, watching him.

Errol shakes his head, closing the bag abruptly.

"A feeling about...the properties of the glass," he explains, a slight frown still on his face. As if something's bugging him, but he can't quite get a handle on it. "My discussions with Bashir have raised questions about the electromagnetic properties of the material. And how we might be able to use that to our advantage."

"Let's get into the rover while we keep talking, guys," Kate interrupts, looking up at the sky uneasily. "I don't know about you, but I want to get back to the city as quickly as possible."

We all murmur our agreement and climb into the rover immediately. She's right. I really don't want to be caught out in another meteor shower. Or have to fend off another attack by Tajss creatures. Yeah, getting going sounds like an excellent plan.

Kate starts up the rover and punches the accelerator before Arawn urges Errol to keep speaking.

"In what way could we use the glass, Errol?" he prompts.

Errol turns in his seat, so he can see both of us and Kate.

"I am not certain," he starts, getting the caveat out from the start. "However, there were stones we once used in our technology. If the meteor glass does indeed have similar electromagnetic properties to those stones..."

"Perhaps they can be used the same way," Arawn finishes quietly.

That gives all of us pause. If Errol is right in his hunch about the glass...

"Do you think that it could be used to restore Tajss? Bring it back to its technological age?" I ask, wanting to be clear about where he's going with this.

"I do not want to make assumptions this early," he says carefully. "However, if my hypothesis is correct...I do not see why not."

"Oh, wow," Kate murmurs. "That's a lot to chew on."

I sit back in my seat in silent agreement and do that.

Chew on it. The implications of that... I can't even fully wrap my head around it without effort. Yes, the Zmaj were obviously a highly technologically advanced civilization, as evidenced by the city and all the impressive aspects of it they're trying to get back on line even now. Like the shield that protects it from the meteor showers and the program that basically uploads linguist information into your brain.

But this could mean more than just extra conveniences or tech that could be really useful to us in day to day life. No, it could mean something even more important. It could mean that space travel might be possible for the Zmaj again, at least at some point. That could be a game changer... Could there be a day where we aren't trapped on Tajss anymore? Where crash-landing here isn't a life sentence not just for us, but for all the generations yet to come?

The idea feels amazing at this point, beyond belief after we've all resigned ourselves to be here for the foreseeable future. However, that doesn't necessarily mean we would go anywhere else. We're building society up again here and with the reintroduction of technology, our lives would likely be even more improved. Less difficult, hopefully.

And who knows what state our initial target planet is in now? Considering that our journey was always set to take multiple generations, that place could be in a different state now. Is the devil we know better than the one that we don't?

And I've just gone from zero to a hundred real fast. I mentally step on the brakes. Probably I should slow down. We need to see if Errol's hunch about the glass is even correct before we start worrying about a decision we may never have to face.

So I take all of my thoughts on the subject and set them aside. We have a lot more immediate matters to worry about. Fortunately, the rest of the journey back is uneventful. After this trip, I'm really looking forward to some good old-fashioned boredom. Interesting is overrated sometimes.

But I can't go turn off my brain just yet. Our first stop upon reaching the city is Rosalind's office. I feel relief flow through me as we step into the protection of the dome, waving at people we see on our walk to Rosalind's building. We're protected from both meteor showers and the beasts on Tajss here. I suppose vulnerability to invader attacks is yet to be seen, but I know we're definitely much safer here than we were in the New Village or traveling. I'll take it.

When we reach Rosalind's office, she sees us right away. Our information is pressing. We need to give her a rundown of everything that happened and of what the miners finally proposed.

"I'm glad you're all back here in one piece," Rosalind greets us, gesturing to the chairs across the desk from her. "Please, have a seat."

Rosalind was and forever will be an intimidating woman. Beautiful and commanding, she's sees everything around her, or at least that's how I've always felt. It can be kind of uncomfortable sometimes, though it's a good quality to have in a leader.

"Did the miners give you any trouble?" Visidion asks as we sit down, his deep green eyes meeting each of ours in turn.

A Commander in his own right, the way he can make you feel as if you're the center of the universe when he locks eyes with you...it's also impressive, a skill that engages anyone. Together, they really are a stellar team. I'm glad we have people like that in charge rather than the weaker leaders we just witnessed at the New Village. To keep this many people in line and working together, you need to be strong. Need to be able to make decisions to help improve our situation even if it means dealing with backlash.

"They weren't happy to see us, if that's what you mean," Kate starts, shaking her head. "You'd think we were there to enslave them or something."

"Though they didn't have any problem taking the supplies you sent with us," I add.

I can't stand hypocrisy. Especially when hate and intolerance is the high horse they've decided to sit on. Rosalind shakes her head, though she doesn't appear surprised at that.

"Typical. You can lead a horse to water..." She sighs, crossing her arms over her chest as Visidion leans against a wall behind her, his eyes watchful.

I have a feeling if anyone makes even a slightly threatening move towards his mate, Visidion will have their head on a platter before they would even know what hit them. I know that Arawn would do the same for me. And isn't that a kicker? I've never had anyone like that in my life. It's...nice. Though that feels like too mild a word for how it feels. Flabbergasting? Amazing? Terrifying?

"True," Kate agrees. "But we did make some progress. Though it wasn't really because of the talks we were having..."

She looks over at Errol.

"What do you mean?" Rosalind asks, leaning forward. "If it wasn't the talks, how did you make any progress?"

"The New Village was attacked," Arawn chimes in.

"Attacked?" Visidion repeats sharply. "By who?"

"By creatures we are not familiar with."

"Creatures that appear to have specifically attacked the New Village in order to kidnap the humans," Errol adds.

Visidion straightens, stepping forward. We have his full attention now.

"To kidnap? Are you certain?"

"We watched them drug a human rather than kill him.

And afterwards, they tied him up. That is not something you do unless you desire to take someone alive," Arawn says.

"Yes," Errol agrees. "And they had on uniforms with a patch that looked oddly familiar, though I couldn't place it..."

Errol reaches into his pack and pulls out one of the patches from the attackers' clothing. He must have taken one for just this purpose. Good call.

When he sets it down on the desk, both Rosalind and Visidion have a visible reaction to it. Visidion's jaw clenches and Rosalind's face hardens. They've seen this patch or symbol before. And it doesn't look like the memories are good ones.

"You know it?" Errol asks, obviously noticing their reactions as well.

"Yes," Rosalind says. "Unfortunately. When the Zzlo kidnapped us, they sold us to people on another planet."

"We saw this symbol there," Visidion says, staring at the patch.

The Zzlo.

The name sends a chill through me. I heard of them after we reconnected with the rest of the people from our ship and the Zmaj. They're bad news.

"The Zzlo are involved in fighting rings, right?" I ask, thinking back to the rumors I've heard. "They kidnap people for the purpose?"

"Yes," Rosalind says, shaking her head. "And nobody wants to be taken by them. Trust me."

As she's had personal experience with the matter, I'll definitely take her word for it. Pursing her lips, she pushes the patch back towards Errol.

"What happened after the attack? I'm assuming you and Arawn were able to fend it off?"

It's a fair assumption, considering we're sitting here.

"Yes," Errol agrees. "It seemed as if the creatures were not expecting to see any Zmaj there."

Visidion smiles, the expression sharp.

"I bet they didn't," he says.

Errol smiles back grimly.

"We caught them by surprise but were only able to kill a few before the rest ran off. We did not pursue for fear of them attacking the New Village while we were gone."

Both Visidion and Rosalind nod, clearly agreeing with the reasoning.

"You did the right thing. I'm assuming the attack was the wakeup call the miners needed?" Rosalind asks.

"In a way," Kate says. "They still do not want an alliance—or at least, they don't want to call it that. But they're willing to exchange the ore they find in the mines for Zmaj protection. At least it's a start."

"And the ore they have could be quite valuable," Arawn says.

"We brought back the samples we traded for." Errol takes out a few different kinds of ore, one that is nearly black and glittery, one that is less opaque, with a subtle sheen, and another that looks to be a pure metal, the glossy shine and the very evenness of it eye catching. "As you can see, these could be quite useful."

"Yes," Visidion says, stepping forward to pick up the smallish pieces, his tone considering. "They could be."

"Worth the protection, huh?" Rosalind asks, staring at the ores. "Not that we wouldn't provide it anyway. I don't like the idea of the miners being so vulnerable to invaders from the space-fighting rings. Nobody deserves to be taken by them and there aren't enough of us to lose even a few." She sighs, leaning back in her seat. "And not that I'm unhappy they've softened their hardline stance. It just isn't ideal that this is what it took."

We all voice our agreement with that.

Begrudging acceptance is better than none.

But it isn't the best foot to start on.

She shakes her head, looking up at Visidion.

"We can't help that, though. We need to send out Zmaj to patrol the New Village as soon as possible. How quickly can we get the discussion going with everyone?"

"Quickly," Visidion says, staring at the ore. "I'll send out messages to everyone immediately."

"Good," Rosalind nods. "Is there anything else you need to tell us?" she asks, returning her attention to our group.

She is clearly already compiling the list of things she needs to get done now that she has this information.

Errol nods.

"Yes. Though it is on an unrelated matter."

Rosalind waves him to continue when he pauses.

"This is more a hypothesis than anything," he starts, similar to how he mentioned his thoughts to us. He wants to manage everyone's expectations, which I understand. "I have been wondering about the electromagnetic properties of the meteorite glass. I think...I believe there is a chance that we could use it to restore some of our old technology," He shifts his eyes from Rosalind's to Visidion's and back. "Especially here in the city, where we have so much at our disposal."

Both of them take a moment to absorb it. They look like they're going through the same thought process we went through.

"Interesting," Visidion murmurs after a few beats. "That is most definitely an avenue we should pursue then. Especially since we seem to have quite an abundance of the material lately," he adds, shaking his head. "The meteor showers are becoming almost commonplace. But perhaps that is not as terrible an occurrence as we all thought."

"Yes," Rosalind agrees. "Very interesting. I think you

should share this idea with those working on the tech currently. See what you can come up with in terms of experimentation."

Errol nods.

"I will do so directly after this meeting."

It doesn't last much longer after that. With all of the pertinent information passed on, we hand over the issue and headache of the New Villagers to Rosalind. I really don't envy her job.

12

ARAWN

"*H*mm. Maybe if we adjust this section here and rotate the glass..." Addison mutters.

"Yes," Errol agrees, reaching out to perform the task, his hands working delicately, careful of sharp edges and fragile sections. "If the meteorite glass has the proper electromagnetic properties, the map should work."

They continue to tinker with it as I and the group working on restoring tech to the city watch.

When Fallon went with Kate to meet with their friends, the females they first arrived in the city with, I decided to go with Errol to see if he is indeed correct about the glass.

When he told Addison about his hypothesis, she'd been excited at the idea, listening intently as Errol explained it.

"We need to see if you're right," she said as soon as he told her. "We've been trying to get some of the other gadgets here working without a whole lot of success. Maybe this is just what we're missing."

The only way to see if the glass could be the missing link for the tech here was to figure out a way to insert it and see if it worked. So they'd decided on a table that could create a three-dimensional, interactive map of the areas around the city. It would work or it wouldn't, and it was one of the simpler pieces. It was also something they felt they could test quickly, or at least what they considered quickly.

The only problem is, the glass isn't the same shape as the stones used to power the tech before. Even if it does have the right properties, it isn't an exact match for whatever was used previously, so adjustments will likely have to be made. All of that means that the test is understandably taking some time.

Addison finally lets out a frustrated huff after about forty minutes.

"Maybe this wasn't the best one to pick," she says, straightening and wiping a hand across her brow. "The glass doesn't want to conform to the space we need it to."

Errol says, "Yes, if there was a quicker way to know if this is even worth our time and energy." He stops talking abruptly and frowns. "Wait. Perhaps we are approaching this incorrectly. There must be a machine here, a scanner to sort through the stones and find the quality ones. I have a vague recollection..." He shakes his head, turning to Addison with renewed energy. "It should be about this big," he explains holding his two fists together. "Made of a hard, shiny material, with a handle on one side, a screen on the other, and a—"

"—funnel-like protrusion on the other side of the screen?" Addison finishes, perking up. "Hold on—I think I might have what you're talking about!"

She hurries away, and we hear her rummaging through a nearby room, muttering to herself. She seems to mutter to herself quite a bit. Perhaps she's spent too much time with the machines rather than people. She is back within a moment, holding out an object that seems like it fits Errol's description quite well. How many objects like that could there be here?

"I found it going through one of the smaller rooms. It seems like it works, but we weren't sure what it was supposed to be for."

She stops talking as the thing lights up in her hand, a blue light shining out from the screen while it emits a mellow beeping sound.

Errol holds out his hand in a silent polite gesture of request, and Addison places the new machine in his grasp. After nodding his formal thanks, Errol moves the object closer to the glass. The beeping intensifies, the blue light shifting to a warm orange.

"I believe we have our answer," Errol says, staring down at the scanner. "The glass contains the properties we need. We simply need to learn how to use it properly."

"Oh, wow!" Addison exclaims, staring at the scanner. "We could do so much! I mean, we still have to figure out how to adjust it properly and so on, but...this could mean bringing everything back! There's so much tech here, so much to revive, to explore." She is almost hopping in her joy, her face aglow with it. "Oh, I have to go tell Rosalind and Visidion—I know they'll want to hear the news right away!" Not waiting for any kind of response, she almost runs from the room, off to deliver the news.

Everyone around me is abuzz with excitement at this confirmation, while Errol continues to tinker with the glass.

I attempt to connect with the atmosphere. I do.

However, I do not feel the same joy, the same excitement everyone else around me seems to be feeling. Frankly, at best, I feel conflicted. Yes, having use of some more of the technology would be wonderful in some ways. I know for a fact life could be made much more convenient. Which I want, both for us and the humans.

A renewal of the technology has other possible ramifications that give me pause. One in particular stands out. This new development could mean a resurrection of the ability to travel into space. Which would in turn make it possible for the humans to leave Tajss.

For Fallon to leave Tajss.

Even just that possibility has me wanting to halt this right here. Not that I could. There is no putting this away now that it is out, now that we've determined the glass could work. Once the kedi is out of the basket, there is no way to make him go back inside, as my mother used to say.

I shake my head, pushing the thought aside. I do not like feeling this way. As though I have to trap Fallon here in order to be with her. I do not want to force her into anything. Do not want her to simply be with me because she is forced to stay. If space travel again becomes a possibility...we will decide what to do when the time comes. Together.

The desire to push the thought aside is tested that evening.

Upon hearing the news that the glass can be used in the tech and the resulting possibilities, Rosalind and Visidion decide to hold a special communal dinner for everyone in the city. Everyone appears to be in their best spirits as the abundance of food and free-flowing drink creates an atmosphere of celebration.

I appreciate it, appreciate the warmth of the dinner, even if I have to set aside my feelings on the matter. It reminds me of those held in the Tribe's caves, like all of us are part of this community, united. There has been a lot to worry about recently and the spirits of those here have felt the burden of that, but the hope sparked by the meteorite glass has everyone buzzing with excitement.

"...and then Errol reminded me of the scanner that we'd set aside because we didn't know what it did. And bam! We had our answer!" Addison recounts once more to her interested audience.

"That's amazing," Sarah murmurs, shaking her head.

"It really is," Kate agrees. "If you hadn't had that hunch, Errol, we may never have realized the glass could be so useful."

Errol shakes his head. "Someone would have thought to check eventually."

"Maybe. Maybe not," Fallon interjects as she leans against my arm, tilting her head to rest it on my shoulder. "Sometimes it's the most obvious things that get overlooked."

I rest my hand on her thigh and she smiles up at me, making no move to hide her affection for me. Actually, she has been openly affectionate towards me all night. Holding my hand, sitting close, rubbing my arm. The open display of connection soothes something inside of me, the part that's been slightly on edge since I realized the possible implications of the glass. She has no problem with people knowing we are together, claiming me in front of them. That gives me a sense of security I appreciate.

"We need to get everything back online if there are going to be more invader attacks. I don't like that they have technology, even rudimentary technology, while we're still trying to play catch up."

"This is true," Drosdan agrees. "Any advantage we can have on our side, we need. Our numbers are simply too small not to gather every resource we can in preparation."

I murmur my agreement with that as Fallon slips her hand into mine. Drosdan is correct. We need the tech. Now that the invaders have seen we are working with the humans, they may come back with greater forces.

As Fallon squeezes my hand, I feel the conflict in me once more, a heaviness that wants to take over. We need the technology. I acknowledge that, admit it. But it may also be the very thing that separates Fallon and me in the future.

I look down at her beloved face, at the light in her eyes as the conversation veers away from the serious topics again and Lanie starts to regale us with kedi stories.

"...and when I woke up, the stuff was everywhere! With Spock in the corner, looking like the cat that stole the canary!"

Fallon laughs, and I take a moment to simply absorb this scene. Absorb her and the easy affection she displays towards me. Now that I have it, that I have her this close to me, not just physically but mentally and emotionally...

My hand tightens on hers. She gives me another smile, shifting to be closer still.

I know that losing her would break me, break me in a way I have not yet experienced.

13

FALLON

The next day, Kate and Errol tell us they need to spend some more time in the city, but Arawn and I are ready to head back to the Tribe's cave system.

Back home.

The city is great, and I like seeing everyone here, but I want to be back where we can be the most comfortable. Where the people who are becoming my family live. It's really nice having a place I actually think of as home.

We were in the tunnels with Annabelle a lot longer than we've been here with the Tribe, but I never thought of them as home, as a place I felt safe. Those tunnels were just a place to exist, a necessary thing to endure if we wanted to survive. Things have changed for the better in a very short amount of time. It's kind of crazy to think of sometimes.

I rub my sweaty face against the shoulder of my shirt as we continue through the desert. Unfortunately, the heat on Tajss is not one of the things that has changed. More's the pity.

Since we decided to head back on our own, and the rover may be needed to transport other people or things, we're traveling the old-fashioned way—on foot. Well, mostly on foot. I've gotten really used to driving, so it's kind of sucking extra hard.

Arawn tightens his hold on my waist. "Are you okay?" he asks, looking down at me as we touch down on the sand once more. He's picked up some human ways of saying things that's really pretty damn adorable. But I might be biased. I think everything about Arawn is adorable.

"Yeah, I'm fine," I reassure him with a smile. "Just hot. But what else is new?"

He smiles back.

"It is not much farther now. We should—" he stops talking and turns his head to the right abruptly. The movement sends a shot of adrenaline through me as I turn to look in the same direction. I didn't hear anything, but I trust Arawn's senses out here a lot more than I trust my own. He's built for this place. When I turn, he is proven right. I see a shadow before I see the beast itself. By this point, I'd know a guster anywhere.

The large lizard is unmistakable even from just a shadow, the humps on its back and the random spikes on its tough skin translate quite readily.

When it rounds the boulder that obscures it from view, it lets out that distinctive growl that somehow manages to blend both the howl of a dog and the hiss of a cat in a spine-tingling sound that just feels wrong.

I stare at the razor-sharp teeth revealed when it opens its mouth and swallow hard, feeling my heart beating fast. Yes, it's scary. It's even scarier because of my past experience with them. I've seen these things kill people viciously, the images, the sheer terror of it, burned into my mind. I've seen the damage they can do. Sometimes, knowledge doesn't give you power. It gives you fear.

I take a deep breath and forcibly steady myself. Cowering

isn't an option. I grip the pole I made sure to bring, but I know the weapon would not be enough to even the playing field between me and that thing. Luckily, I'm not alone.

"Stay here," Arawn orders, letting go of me and stepping away, bringing his lochaber around in a two-handed grip.

He doesn't wait for me to acknowledge the order, simply leaps towards the beast that obviously has its eyes set on us, his wings helping him float over the distance.

I know he's facing the thing head on for me. I know if he was traveling alone, he might have outrun the thing rather than expend energy killing it. But with me along, he has to take care of the threat because I slow him down.

All right. I grip the pole between my hands and watch, ready to intervene with whatever strength and skill I can muster if Arawn needs help. It might not be much in comparison to him, but a well-placed poke could be enough to distract the thing long enough so he can make the kill.

But as I watch Arawn leap into the air, his tail whipping out behind him, his wings flared out to give his leap an added lift, the sun gleaming off the blade of his lochaber, I realize he's not going to need my help after all.

The guster shifts at the last moment and Arawn's blade sinks into its tough back rather than at the base of the skull like he was aiming for, but he turns it to his advantage. Using the handle to steady himself, he lands on the beast's bucking back. I don't know how he manages to stay on it.

I take a step forward, heart in my throat as I see the thing twist its head back in an almost boneless maneuver, its jaws open wide as it tries to snap at Arawn. If it manages to get ahold of him, I know for a fact its bite strength is powerful enough to cut him in half.

I've seen it.

But Arawn shifts out of the way smoothly and yanks the blade out of the animal, and when the guster turns again to try to chomp down on him, he's ready with his weapon. With a grunt of effort, he jams the blade right through that open mouth, his body twisting hard to move fast and powerfully. The blade goes right through the back of the guster's throat. Arawn jerks the blood-covered blade to the side in a hard wrench, severing the spinal cord.

The guster dies instantly.

I stare, trying to process the fact that he already won. Arawn pulls out his weapon and leaps off the thing's back as it falls to the ground, limp. My heart is still racing as I look down at the felled beast.

Well...shit.

Arawn steps forward and wipes his bloody blade on the animal's now still side, barely out of breath. The fight was quick and harsh.

"Uh..." I swallow, taking a step closer. "Should we break it down for meat?" I ask, clearing my throat as my voice comes out slightly squeaky. Trying to sound normal because he looks so unfazed. Arawn shakes his head, turning back towards me.

"No. We are near enough to the caves that we can send a group out here to retrieve the meat. I do not want to stay out here with you any longer unless absolutely necessary." He scans the horizon. "There is no reason to take the risk."

Yeah, I'm completely okay with that. So I lean against Arawn as he wraps his arm around my waist once more and uses his wings to help us skim across the sand.

I tighten my grip on him, still processing. I shudder a little as I think about what would have likely happened had I been alone. Yeah, I might have made the guster work a bit for its meal. But there's no doubt in my mind that it would have been successful in the end. I just don't have the reflexes, the speed, or the power that Arawn has. Or the other Zmaj do.

It galls a bit, knowing I simply don't have the freedom to

travel across the desert on my own, due to safety issues. But reality is what it is. And I'd rather be alive than try to prove any kind of nebulous point. I'm also fortunate enough that I don't have to travel the desert on my own in any case, so why borrow trouble when I have enough already on my plate?

When the cave system comes into view, along with the protective wall, I breathe a sigh of relief. Home and safety. I'll never take it for granted, not here on Tajss.

Hell, I never really had it on the ship either. Not with the family I was stuck with—or lack thereof.

"Home sweet home," I say quietly.

"Yes," Arawn agrees simply. "I am glad to be back."

That makes two of us.

When we walk in, we're greeted by everyone with hugs and questions about our trip. We've arrived a bit before everyone would be finishing up work to take part in the communal meal, but they decide to put things down a little early, excited to catch up with us.

"What was the New Village like?" Delilah asks.

"Is Jackson still at the helm?" Bashir chimes in.

"Did they come to their senses and decide to ally with us?" Padraig questions, his tone scathing.

"Jackson's still in charge," I answer first. "Though vocal minority is definitely something to watch out for." Bashir nods, frowning. "And I guess they came to their senses a bit, though it did take more than we'd hoped..."

I look back at Arawn.

"There was an attack on the village," he explains baldly.

"An attack?" Bashir asks, his voice sharp. "By a beast of some kind?"

If only it were so simple.

"No," Arawn says. "By a foreign group there to kidnap the humans. The emblem they wore made it clear they were connected to a planet the Zzlo do business with. That was confirmed by both Rosalind and Visidion when they were shown a patch Errol collected from one of the bodies."

That sends everyone into a tailspin. I totally understand. This threat wasn't even on my radar before.

"Kidnappers? Shit."

"I've heard of the fighting rings. Bad news."

"Obviously you were able to fight them off. But will they be back?"

"Wait, so the villagers finally realized how vulnerable they are? This is what it took!?"

Arawn holds up a hand and the buzz of conversation dies down slowly.

"The villagers did indeed realize the exact extent of their vulnerability," Arawn acknowledges. "This is why they offered a trade—Zmaj protection in exchange for the ore they are digging up from the mines."

"Rosalind is figuring out patrols right now," I add. "She doesn't want to leave them vulnerable any longer than strictly necessary."

That sends people off again. Obviously, this is something that will affect us here too, if the Zmaj have to take turns going out to the New Village to provide that protection. That means putting themselves in the way of danger. Both in the journey and if there's an actual attack.

I understand having mixed feelings about that, especially when the Zmaj will be protecting people with deeply seated xenophobic views. Putting your life on the line for people who don't want you to mix with their race...yeah, that isn't ideal.

Needless to say, the attack and the village as well as the resulting exchange is the hot topic of conversation during dinner. Though I also notice people aren't ignorant to the change between Arawn and me. We sit together, which is a clear change from before.

We are obviously a lot closer and a lot more comfortable with one another, touching casually, leaning against each other. Though, admittedly, the change is me. Arawn would have liked to be this close well before my own change of heart. I almost can't remember why I was so resistant to the idea. It seems so stupid now.

When I nudge Arawn, wanting to leave the dinner, I see Delilah and Nora give each other a knowing look. Yeah, I know how it looks. Fuck it. I don't care if everyone sees.

Now that I'm not resisting Arawn, I feel like I can't keep my hands off him, and I don't want to try. Luckily, it sure looks like he feels the same. He constantly has a hand resting on my thigh, an arm wrapped around my waist or shoulders, or is holding my hand in a warm, comforting clasp. He wants to touch me as much as I want to touch him. It feels really good to be so wanted.

"You would like to retire?" he asks, turning to me immediately.

I nod. "I'm tired. Where do you want to go? Your cave or mine?" I never thought those particular words would ever come out of my mouth. Especially not referring to caves. Sometimes I feel like I'm living in a weird alternate reality where I'm becoming a Flintstone. Maybe I should tie a guster bone into my hair. Start a new trend.

Arawn smiles. "Mine has more space," he says immediately. "And my pallet is larger."

Can't argue with that. It has to accommodate his body, after all.

"Okay. Your cave it is."

So we say our goodbyes, ignoring the looks we get, and head back to Arawn's cave.

"Are you very tired?" Arawn asks once we're alone, wrapping his arms around me and pulling me in close to his hard body. Hard in more ways than one. I can feel exactly how "not tired" he is, right up against my front.

"I'm not *that* tired," I respond, rubbing against him lightly.

"Hmm. Good."

I'm smiling as his mouth comes down on mine and he shifts us over to the pallet. It's thick and plush, cradling my body perfectly as Arawn gets to work. By the time he's done getting out all that energy, I'm ready to pass out like a baby. I turn and kiss his warm neck, snuggling into him and closing my eyes as he holds me close. I'm asleep before I know it. Who needs sleeping pills? I sleep deeply, not stirring at any point.

Waking up the next morning is just as great. I could really get used to waking up with Arawn's body wrapped around me.

"Morning," I murmur, turning in his arms to kiss his chin, his cheeks, his lips.

"Hmm."

We stay like that for a little longer than I normally would, snuggled together in the warm nest of his pallet. I don't usually have such a good incentive to delay the start of the day.

When we do finally get up—keeping in mind that we have duties to fulfill, now that we're back—and walk over to the bulletin board hand in hand, I'm a little surprised to see that the tasks we're assigned for the day have more than a little overlap. I'll be seeing Arawn throughout, as if we're already mated. Our interaction last night was definitely noticed. Not that I didn't know that before, but this concrete change is still a little surprising. Especially so fast.

Arawn makes a pleased sound. "Good. It seems as though our first tasks will take us both to the kitchen," he murmurs.

"Yeah."

And you know what? Spending so much time with Arawn

during the day sounds great to me. Maybe I should be wary of spending that much time with him so fast, but I'm not. I'd be happy to spend the whole day and night with him, honestly.

Oh, man. I'm becoming one of those people who made me want to gag before. If I start mentioning Arawn in every sentence, I'm going to have to smack myself. But it doesn't seem to matter that I know I'm becoming that person.

Despite those thoughts, I float through the day, touching Arawn whenever I see him, sitting with him at lunch time. Seeing the heat in his eyes as the day goes by. The same heat that I feel rising inside me.

By the time the communal dinner comes around, we're both more than ready to be alone again.

To that end, we eat quickly, trying to finish this last task.

"Slow down—don't choke on it!" Delilah laughs as she sees me shoving food into my mouth. "Trust me—Arawn won't start without you."

"Uh huh," I agree. Yep, I'm completely shameless.

He's sitting not that far away, done with his food and ostensibly watching a checkers match.

But I feel his eyes on me the entire time, so I don't think he's really keeping up with whatever's happening with the game. His mind is on something else entirely.

I swallow, feeling myself blush a bit. Okay, maybe not completely shameless.

"Well, I don't want to take that chance," I shoot back with a grin as I clean up my plate. "See you later."

I can hear her laughing behind me as I get up and walk over to Arawn. At least I'm a good source of amusement.

He's already up and ready to go before I reach him, plainly sitting there just to wait for me. We leave hand in hand. I almost float back into his cave, anticipation building inside me. We're definitely in the honeymoon phase of a new relationship.

Though, if I think about it...all of the Zmaj-human couples I see don't seem that far removed from how we're feeling. It's an interesting realization, but I don't have much time to dwell on it.

As soon as we're alone once more, we strip and drop down to the pallet, completely in sync. As I kiss him, smooth my hands over his skin, over the delicate bones in his wings, I wonder how long we'll feel like this. How long we won't be able to keep our hands off of each other.

Months?

Years?

Forever?

I might die, but I'm not mad at the thought.

Arawn rolls me onto my back as I'm ruminating over that, pushing my legs apart with his heavy thigh. Breaking the kiss, he props himself up on his arms, his eyes scanning me. I feel my face and chest flush under his regard.

"You are so soft," he croons, cupping a breast in one large hand. "So beautiful."

"I feel beautiful. With you," I confess.

I've never felt so desirable. So completely feminine.

He leans down to kiss me, my hips cradling his as his erection slides against me. Hot and hard, it feels amazing.

"Good."

The way he touches me, looks at me...I can't get enough. We devour each other again. My sleep is just as deep. The next morning is the same as the one before. Arawn's arms are starting to feel like the place I should be always.

It would scare me if I had some distance. So much desire, so much want for someone else...It makes you vulnerable. But I don't have any distance. I'm right in the thick of it. And what would worrying accomplish anyway? I'm already in too deep.

The next few days pass in the same rosy, delicious haze. We spend the day taking care of tasks that have us interacting regularly. We have all our meals together. And as soon as the suns set, we can't keep our hands off each other. The day ends. And then we wake up together to start all over again.

It's almost...perfect. But perfection isn't real. It never lasts forever. It can't. Reality eventually intrudes. It doesn't take long before something introduces a sour note into our idyllic routine.

It happens on a morning like the last few, with Arawn and me cuddling before we absolutely have to get up and get started with our day. I feel warm and relaxed. Arawn cups the side of my face, his eyes tracing my features. I'm getting used to seeing the love in them. Love directed at me.

"You are so lovely. I sometimes imagine how adorable our children will be because of you."

My smile fades, and a stab of real fear hits me, shaking me right out of my relaxed state. Like someone just dumped a bucket of ice-cold water over me. I pull back reflexively, unable to help my reaction.

I know he didn't mean to alarm me. I don't think it even entered my mind that it could be a sensitive subject. But even the casual mention of children—our children—has my emotions immediately entering a tail spin. I need some distance, some space to process all of this.

"Is something wrong?" Arawn asks, frowning as I sit up.

"No," I reassure him, trying a smile. I know it isn't very convincing when his look of worry only intensifies. "Uh, we should probably get started with the work we need to get done today," I offer lamely as I climb to my feet.

I can't think of a better, more natural way to get away. I

grab my clothes and start dressing quickly. I feel like the walls are closing in on me. I need air.

"Are you certain nothing is wrong?" Arawn asks again, getting to his feet as well, reaching out to turn me around with a gentle hand on my arm.

"No, I'm fine," I say again, patting his hand and slipping out of his hold in the same move. "I'll see you out there, all right?"

And then I'm out of his cave, avoiding looking at his face. Avoiding whatever I'm making him feel. Like a coward. But I'm spooked. Beyond spooked. And the kicker is...I don't really even know why. Why did that casual comment hit me so hard?

As we go through the day, I maintain my distance from Arawn despite running into him constantly due to our assigned tasks. An irritation now, where it felt like a wonderful perk before.

I can see his confusion, his hurt as I avoid lingering around him, keeping everything business only. But I feel like I need that distance to try to process this aversion I feel at the thought of children with him. It's perplexing, to say the least. In complete contradiction to the feelings I have for my sweetheart of a warrior, the deeper instincts he's uncovered in me.

To add to the mess, I feel a sense of panic at my own distress. I know I could lose him if I don't have his children, if I don't agree to mate him. I know that. Know how important both mating and family are to the Zmaj.

But even though I know that risk, I still can't shake this fear, this sense of being trapped. I never wanted children, it's true. I never played house, pretended to have a family of my own like some of the other girls my age did. It just wasn't me. I never even expected to be in a long-term, committed relationship.

But here I am now. In love. Facing the very real prospect of eventually mothering Arawn's children. And the idea is killing me. What's wrong with me? And what am I going to do?

That night, I eat quickly once more. But not because I want to be alone with Arawn like before. When he stands along with me, I shake my head.

"I'm...I'm going to go back to my cave," I say in a low voice, cognizant of all the ears likely listening around us. "I'm sorry...I'm just tired."

It sounds like a lie even to me. But there's no way to make it sound like anything else.

"I... see." Arawn slowly sits back down, his face clearing of emotion. Hiding what he's feeling. "Perhaps I will see you in the morning?"

I nod, tossing him a brief smile.

"Sure."

But then I hurry away without another word. And I feel terrible about it. That night leads to more nights I spend away from him. And more days where I minimize contact.

I know it isn't fair to him. Know that I'm hurting him when he doesn't deserve to be hurt. Know that I risk losing him, not just because of this distance I'm creating, but also because of this outright fear I have of children. Of continuing his line.

But I don't know what else to do.

How can I fix this?

Can I fix this?

14

ARAWN

"We cannot be unprepared with the threat of invaders a reality," Kalessin announces to the assembled Zmaj. "That is why we have called you together here today."

"We must spar and hone our skills in order to be prepared for any eventuality," Falkosh adds. "To that end, we have arranged to include such sessions into your schedules for the week." He pauses, his lips pressing into a thin line. "We must be ready. There is no other option."

The Tribe elders are correct. Hunting is not enough to keep our fighting skills at their peak conditions. Fighting an intelligent opponent is different from felling a beast.

"Your session times have been posted," Kalessin informs us. "Check to see when you are scheduled."

We make our way over to the schedule, passing by it in an orderly line.

"It seems as though we are sparring first," Bashir murmurs after we look at the schedule.

I nod. They have staggered these sessions, alternating people to sharpen skills so that the work that needs to be done for day-to-day life can still be accomplished. Life will not pause simply because a new threat looms.

Bashir and I square off that day. I examine myself critically. I feel that my reflexes are just a hair slower than they could be, my strategic brain not quite as quick as I wish. Bashir voices the same.

"It is good we have these sessions now to improve," he says after we break, both of us breathing hard. "I did not even realize I had softened."

"Yes," I agree. "Even if the invaders don't attack, it will keep us in good shape for any possibility."

He voices his approval of that.

After we catch our breath, we reengage, as our session is not yet over. As I turn to parry a blow, I catch sight of Fallon peeking around the corner into the large cavern we are using for these sparring and practice meetings. I fumble the move and Bashir succeeds in pinning me.

"Pay attention!" Kalessin barks out when he sees the mistake.

With a growl, I rise back to my feet, glancing over where I caught that brief glimpse of Fallon.

She is gone.

My stomach drops once more. I do not know why she has withdrawn from me so abruptly after we had made such progress. But I do know I am losing my patience with her distancing. Is this how she will always react?

I put all my frustration and anger into the sparring session, pushing Bashir back, his eyes widening at the renewed onslaught. I am utterly unsure of how to approach the emotions of human females. They are a mystery that I am obviously not so adept at understanding. Why does Fallon give and then retreat? Is it something I do or is it something else entirely? Did I say something that upset her?

My thoughts have been spinning out of control every

night as I comb through our interactions again and again, attempting to understand what may have triggered her withdrawal and only frustrating myself further.

Every time I think on it, I inevitably come back to the fact that she withdrew directly after I mentioned children. But that makes absolutely no sense to me, so I keep looking for another reason.

Feinting to the right, I brace myself with my lochaber and sweep Bashir's legs out from under him, flipping the lochaber around and swinging the bladed end down. I pause with it an inch away from his vulnerable throat.

"Good! Very good, Arawn!" Kalessin calls out. "You have proven yourself able and fit, indeed."

I nod at the elders watching over the sessions, feeling the words bolster my confidence. I have rarely disappointed the elders with my abilities or actions. At least they approve of me.

I sigh internally. My confidence has definitely taken a blow from Fallon's actions. Why would she not want to have my children? Am I not a good protector? Not a good provider? Does she not like who I am as a person? Does she think I would not be a good father?

I reach down to help Bashir to his feet. He is not nearly as enthusiastic about the defeat, scowling at me.

"I will defeat you next time, Arawn."

"You may try," I goad him with a smirk, though my attention is not even fully on him.

It is on Fallon. As it has been on her since she distanced herself, worrying at the problem. Feeling the cold chill of the loss of her. I watch for her throughout the rest of the practice, but she does not reappear.

I know I will see her again, as our tasks are still set in order to see each other throughout the day. It is a torture of a specific kind to see but be unable to touch her. Unable to speak to her past the pleasantries she has kept our conversation to. But that does not mean I do not want to keep torturing myself in exactly that manner. I would rather see her than not see her at all, despite the pain it brings me.

The elders finally call a halt to the practice just as Padraig hurries over to them, a message clutched in hand. We all pause to watch as Kalessin reads the missive, a frown marring his face.

What could it be? Messages like this only come from the city...

Our questions are answered almost immediately. He looks up after scanning the words, his eyes troubled.

"It is a message from Rosalind. She needs more Zmaj to send to the New Village."

The news isn't completely unexpected, but it still sends a ripple of unease through us.

"We will speak and decide on who to send," Falkosh says into the uneasy silence. "You may go about your day."

With that clear dismissal, we break apart and do just that. Patrolling the New Village is going to change our way of life, but it is a necessary change. In the meantime, all of us still have duties to fulfill.

My next stop is Errol's workshop, where I am tasked with gathering more meteorite glass to transport to the city. With the discovery of what the meteorite glass could potentially do, the city needs as much of it as it can get to continue experimentation and hopefully bring a larger percentage of the technology back on line. Errol drove back for just that reason.

"How much of the glass we have gathered are we taking to the city?" I ask as we pack it up carefully.

We want to keep each piece as intact as possible. If they need to break the larger ones into smaller pieces, that will be easy enough with the judicial application of force.

But it would require a lot more effort to figure out a way to meld small pieces back together in a way that doesn't change the properties of the glass itself.

"Most of it," Errol says. "We will keep a small portion in case we need it in the future, but the city has much more use for it now. I have spoken with the Elders, and they agree with my assessment."

I nod. That makes sense. We know Rosalind will send help if we need it. She has proven that she cares about the whole, all of the communities, not just about the city where she lives. We all need to continue to work together as we grow.

I do not want the next generation to grow up in a Tajss where we have petty bickering and fighting among the different communities we have managed to build so far.

I feel a stab of pain at the thought of the next generation. But more because it reminds me of Fallon. I want children, though I want her more. However, I still don't understand why she is so set against the idea.

"I will go take this batch to the rover while you continue packing," Errol informs me. "I believe that will be the last pallet," he adds, eyeing the amount with a critical eye.

"I will join you with it as soon as I am done."

Errol lifts his pallet with a grunt of effort—each individual piece of glass is not heavy, but the combined weight of this much is quite a lot—and leaves to pack it into the rover along with the rest that we have already set inside.

The vehicle Kate engineered has seen a lot of use. Perhaps in the future, once we have our tech back online, we can figure out a way to create more such vehicles. I consider that as I wrap the last piece of glass. I am setting it onto my pallet when I hear running footsteps outside.

I look up quickly.

Is something wrong?

I feel a surge of energy go through me as I grab my lochaber, worried we might be under attack.

I've taken only one step towards the door leading out when Fallon bursts in, her face drawn with fear.

"What is it?" I ask, quickly circling around her to guard her back from whatever threat sent her to flee, my lochaber held tightly in my grip. "Who is chasing you?"

My lochaber stays by my side at all times. With the addition of the new threat of invaders, I feel ill-prepared without it.

"Nobody is chasing me," Fallon gasps, still catching her breath.

What? I turn to her, confused.

"Nobody is chasing you?" I repeat. "Then why are you running?"

She stares at me, her face flushed with exertion. Swallowing, she breaks eye contact, her attention going towards the pallet, packed neatly.

"Where are you going?" she asks, rather than answering my question.

"To the city. To deliver more meteorite glass from Errol's workshop," I add. "Why?"

"I heard...I heard that Rosalind sent for more Zmaj," she admits, meeting my eyes once more. "I... came to check on you."

Ah.

My grip loosens on the lochaber as I relax, and hope grows in my chest.

"Worried about me?" I tease gently, not wanting to embarrass her.

And so glad she still feels for me. Nobody would look that genuinely frightened unless they cared. Distance or no. Fallon nods, not denying it.

"I'm sorry, Arawn," she says in a low voice.

I know she is not apologizing simply for running in here in a panic. But now is not the time to speak on this, not while Errol is waiting for me.

I smile at her, wanting to hug her, hold her close and reassure both of us. But not knowing if that is something I can do just yet.

"I will be back in the evening," I say instead. "Perhaps we can speak then?"

"Yeah. Yeah, okay," she agrees, relief clear in her expression and her voice. "I'll see you then."

"Yes."

Nothing will keep me from her. Not knowing how else to end this, I pick up the pallet and nod at her before stepping out. I want to stay, fix this now, but it will be better to do so when we have more time, when we can properly air everything.

So I go to the rover with the pallet, even though I want to turn around and pull Fallon into my arms and make everything better. I did not like seeing her so frightened, however, that fear was what finally drove her to me, forced her to admit that she cares.

"What are you smiling about?" Errol asks as I set the pallet on top of the others. "This is not that pleasant of a job," he quips.

"Nothing," I say, rounding the vehicle and slipping into the rover. "Nothing at all."

Errol clearly does not believe me, but he only shakes his head and sits down as well.

I cannot help my buoyant spirits. If Fallon fears for my life, she is not going anywhere, despite her withdrawal. And I know I want her with me for always. I want to announce that we are together, want to mate her officially, before everyone's eyes, so there is no confusion about us.

When we arrive at the city, I am still thinking about her

and what I want. I want to keep her safe. I want to provide her with everything she could ever need. Want to give her everything she desires.

People come out to help us unload the rover while I'm still thinking of everything I want in the future, Addison chattering excitedly.

"Oh, this is wonderful! We have so much to test things out now! Thanks for bringing this, guys!"

"Of course," Errol replies. "I want us to have the best chance of finding how to use the glass as well."

Addison grins, her excitement palpable as she sees the massive amount of glass. But not everyone in the city is feeling so joyful.

As we carry the glass throughout the city, dropping pieces off in different locations to use for different tech, we catch snippets of the conversation going on. And it is not all good. In fact, most of it is bad.

"Is it a good idea to send so many Zmaj to the New Village? What if the invaders decide to attack us? We need to keep as many here as possible."

"Yeah, I think you're right. But you know Rosalind—always looking at the long game. And we need to have everyone for that, to be at our strongest..."

"Do we have a contingency plan if we are attacked? What if one of us is taken before anyone realizes? Shouldn't we have some kind of roll call or something to keep track of our numbers?"

"...I heard they sell people to fighting rings. Like we're animals! Man, I don't know..."

"...How can we even successfully repel a full invasion? So far, it's just been small groups. But if they get their shit together and come *en masse*...we just don't have the numbers to hold them off."

"We need to spend more time fortifying the city rather

than spending resources bringing random tech back online. If we're attacked, who cares what cool gadgets we have..."

I hear all of it, and I understand the worry, the fear. Understand why they speak of the prospect of doom.

They are right to worry. I feel the threat as well. But I am confident in my abilities. Confident that I can keep Fallon safe. Determined that no harm will befall her no matter what happens. I simply need to convince her of our mating, so I can forever keep her protected. I hold on to that thought as we climb back into the rover and start our journey back to the Tribe's caves.

I will have Fallon.

And I will keep her safe.

15

FALLON

I finish picking the vegetables we need for dinner that night and stand up, arching my back and rubbing at the base of my spine to relieve the tension there.

Twisting and bending to pick everything is no joke.

I'm glad we alternate tasks.

"I'm just going to go deliver this to kitchen and then I'll be back," I tell Nora.

"All right," she acknowledges, wiping the sweat from her brow. "Man, I'm never going to get used to this heat."

"Yeah," I agree, sighing.

The hats we wear protect us from the sun, but there really isn't anything to protect us from the heat. Hey, maybe if we can use the meteor glass to get the tech back online, we can rig some kind of climate control. A girl can hope. It would be heavenly to not sweat buckets every day.

I start walking towards the kitchen, my mind turning to Arawn as it always seems to do when I'm not fully occupied with a task. I'm glad we're going to talk when he gets back.

The sheer terror I felt when I thought he was going to be riding off into danger at Rosalind's call. Well. Let's just say it was a wakeup call of my own. I don't want to lose Arawn. The thought of him getting hurt, or not coming back at all...it really put our relationship into perspective.

I want to make it work. Want to figure out how we can be together so we both have what we need. I hope we can talk this through. That's my goal. I want him in my life for good.

I frown as I hear an odd sound while I walk. Is someone working on the wall again? I turn to look in that direction as I hear it once more. An odd staccato sound that—

My stomach drops as I turn fully towards the wall.

Shit.

I drop the basket and start running away from the sound, not wanting to be weighed down.

"Attack!" I shout as loudly as my lungs can handle. "Invaders! We're under attack!"

I hear the sound again and look over my shoulder just as one of those odd-looking gray-blue brutes that attacked the New Village climbs over the top. It opens its mouth to emit that odd, distinctive roar again, displaying razor-sharp teeth.

Shit!

I turn back around to yell again, but I don't have to. All of the Zmaj are already streaming out of the caves, weapons in hand as they run towards the wall.

"Stay back!" Melchior yells at me as he passes.

Yeah, that seems like a good plan. At least until I get my hands on my pole.

I don't know how many are out there, how many they've decided to attack our cave system with. If they've spent any time watching and preparing, they'll know there's a sizable Zmaj population here, which means won't be surprised to see them like they were at the New Village. It also means they may have come with a significantly larger number.

Shit shit shit.

Bailey and Astrid come out and run alongside me, Delilah trailing us.

"Going to get your weapons?" Delilah asks us.

"Yeah."

"Yup."

"That's my goal."

"Good," she says with a grim smile. "We need to be prepared to fight."

Glad we're all on the same page.

As I run to my cave and grab my pole, I make a note to myself. I need to keep it with me like Arawn does with his lochaber. I've gotten complacent here in the Tribe's cave system, too accustomed to the safety that I expect to find here.

I feel the back of my neck tingle as I turn to run back out of my cave, overwhelmed with the realization that the conditions here on Tajss might be getting worse. Worse for a while.

If invaders like these are the new normal...we're going to have to make some real adjustments. But that's something to figure out later. You know—when we're not in the middle of a full-blown attack.

I hustle out at that thought. When I make it back to the wall—which is doing its job, as it's slowing down the influx of the attackers, but is really geared more towards protecting us from the larger predators—the Zmaj are doing a heck of a job fighting back. Not surprising.

I've been privy to their fighting skills more than once, and I'm glad that they're on our side. But as good as they are, as I feared, the invaders came in a larger group this time. A much larger group.

"One of those things is going to get through," Delilah mutters next to me.

More than one if they keep coming like this.

"They won't get through us," I say grimly, tilting the pole down so the pointed end is aimed forward.

"Fuck," Nora mutters next to me, doing the same.

All the women slowly show up, and seeing us, take the same stance. Until there's a line of us just waiting, sharp ends lined up in preparation. We don't have to wait long.

The first one breaks through and rushes towards us, angling its tusks down. He doesn't make it far. Not with multiple poles spearing right into him at once. By the end, he's basically shish kebab.

"Here comes another one!"

I look up as I brace my foot on the body, yanking back with all of my strength to dislodge my weapon. Luckily, there are others ready and waiting to take care of the new guy.

"Come on," I mutter to myself. Adrenaline gives me the strength I need to yank it free finally.

"Eeew," I grimace at the squelching sound it makes.

It's definitely different killing something that isn't an animal. I know that these things are sentient, that they have a higher level of thinking. I've never seen a guster in a uniform.

"No time to be a princess about it, Fallon," Delilah barks. "Here's another one!"

She's right. There's no time to dwell on it. Not with a steady trickle of the things getting through the Zmaj warriors, despite their best efforts.

Soon, I'm not thinking of anything. Just stabbing. Stab. Pull free. Reposition. Stab again.

The scent of blood and gore is ripe even though we're in the back, where most of the bodies are not. The Zmaj are taking care of the vast majority out there.

Gritting my teeth, I'm pulling my pole out of yet another body when I hear a new commotion on the other side of the wall.

Less than a minute later, Errol and Arawn leap over the wall and land on our side. Arawn's eyes find me quickly, scanning me to make certain I'm all right. I do the same, relieved to see him back in one piece.

Now, to just keep it that way. The two of them turn swiftly, lochabers in hand. They cut the number getting through to us by almost a hundred percent. I watch, even more in awe of Arawn's prowess now that I've had to work with multiple other people to be a fraction as effective.

His lochaber swings tirelessly, his wings flaring to help him leap and attack invaders at the top of the wall, before they can even climb over, his tail whipping furiously behind him. The muscles of his arms and back bunch and ripple with his movements, the power in his body obvious.

I find myself staring at him more than I probably should be when I need to be keeping an eye out for those of our enemies that get through them. There are much longer breaks now between those that get through. But they do keep coming.

We get to a point where I start to wonder if there's a never-ending swarm of these guys and how long we can hold them off, when something big slams directly into the wall.

At first, I think one of the Zmaj just threw one of the smaller invaders. It's been happening. But then something whizzes by my ear and slams into the ground just feet away, the heat of fire unmistakable. It crushes one of the things about to attack, dropping it to the ground instantly. Huh. That was convenient.

"Meteor storm!" someone who I can't see yells out loud. "Get to cover!"

On the heels of that yell, I hear a shrill, alien scream. By the way I see the six-armed beings turn tail and run, I'm guessing that scream was their leader basically telling them the same.

In one bound, Arawn is next to me, wrapping an arm around my waist in a firm grip.

"Hold on!" he orders.

I clamp my arms around him and he leaps the distance to the nearest cave. All around us, Zmaj do the same with the other women, everyone trying to get to cover as quickly as possible. Most of us end up in one of the communal caves, still breathing hard, the heat of battle very real.

"Are you hurt?" Arawn asks, letting go of me to look me up and down.

I shake my head no.

"Are you hurt anywhere?" I ask, turning the question back on him.

"Only bruises and minor injuries," he reassures me.

When I look him over, I see he's telling the truth. There are a few places where I think the blood is his, but even I can tell the wounds are shallow.

"The meteor shower has ended the battle and given us a reprieve," Falkosh announces, projecting his voice over the multiple conversations happening around us. He waits until everyone quiets down and gives him their attention before continuing. "It would be prudent of us to convene and discuss strategies to prevent being taken unawares in the future." He pauses, looking around at us. "We should have done this as soon as we heard of the new threat. My apologies for not meeting on the matter before it came to us in such an undeniable manner."

What he's saying makes a lot of sense. We should all have a meeting about this.

Unfortunately, it becomes quite clear that he doesn't mean all of us as the Zmaj immediately separate themselves from the rest of us humans and sit down in the back.

Really?

I take a step closer, trying to hear the low-voiced conversation they start.

"Once the meteor shower is over, the first order of business will be to meet with Rosalind on the matter. We need to work together on this..."

I take another step closer, but my forward momentum is abruptly stopped with a strong hand on my arm.

"Let them work it out," Delilah orders, not unkindly. "We don't have nearly the same experience or knowledge of Tajss that they do. And I don't know about you, but I'm starving after all of that. We're better off using this time to get dinner going than basically just sitting and listening to them talk."

I don't know about that. And I have to say, retreating to the kitchen with the other women kind of offends my sensibilities. Not that Delilah isn't right, at least practically speaking.

Okay, fine. If I feel like the plan they come up with needs adjusting, I'll just voice my opinion after we hear it. Nobody will be able to keep my mouth shut.

So I go to the kitchen and help out, feeling my stomach grumble as I do. I guess I am hungry. We throw together something quick, easy, and filling. Nobody has the patience or energy for anything fancy. The smell of the food is enough to have the group of Zmaj trailing out from the strategy meeting to eat.

Arawn finds me and sits down next to me for the meal, everything that has been left unsaid still between us. Yes, we care about each other. Both of our actions say that pretty loud and clear. But we still need to talk.

"What are you doing after this?" I ask as I take another bite of the food.

"I am collecting more meteorite glass along with some of the others. It only makes sense to fill the rover with as much as we can before we send a messenger to inform Rosalind of the attack. Especially when she and her people will be borrowing the rover to deliver her chosen patrols to the New Village."

"I'm coming with you," I say. "To collect the glass."

Arawn frowns. "You do not have to take part in this extra duty."

"I want to."

After everything that has happened...I want to be next to Arawn, just to reassure myself. He must see that I really need this, so he doesn't argue with me again. Simply nods.

We finish our meal and then head right out. Now that the meteor shower is over, there's actually plenty of glass to collect nearby. At least something good comes out of each of these things.

I do find myself more paranoid than usual as we gather the still warm glass though, looking over my shoulder at every noise, afraid it's an indication of another attack.

"Do not worry," Arawn murmurs from next to me when I do it for the third or fourth time. "I am keeping watch."

I nod, giving him a tense smile, but it does help me relax a bit. It also helps that the bodies of the invaders have already been carted off where they won't attract any unwanted wildlife. We're lucky we got off so lightly. There were some of us that sustained some minor injuries, but no casualties.

Not that we can get complacent, but I was so happy to hear that after the fight was over. I'm also happy we're not out in the open collecting glass for long. With a group of us all working together, we make quick work of packing the rover to capacity.

"I think that is all it can take," Bashir comments, patting the rover. "Time to drive it to the city."

We voice our goodbyes as he climbs in and starts his journey. With that done, there is nothing left to do but retire to our cave for the night. Our cave. My cave hasn't felt quite like home after I spent even those few nights with Arawn in his. I think it's more a function of him not being there than the actual space itself. I missed him. Badly.

Arawn doesn't say anything as we walk together in silent agreement. But once we're alone, I know we have to start. I rub my hands on my pants as I turn towards him. I am really not looking forward to this. So I delay it.

"Let me just help you clean up first..."

Going over to the water and cloths he keeps for washing up in one corner, I bring them both back and clean his injuries. They aren't bad, so it really doesn't take long as he stands there quietly, allowing me to do so.

Then I have no excuses left. I stand up, taking the supplies back. Then I turn around to face him again.

"So..." I start, crossing my arms in what I know is a defensive gesture. But I just can't help it.

How the hell do I say this?

"I'm afraid to have children," I blurt out.

All righty then. That's one way of doing it. At least I got it out.

Arawn frowns, taking a stool and dropping down on it.

"Why?" he asks simply.

"I don't know," I start, combing my hair off my face as I start to pace in front of him. "There are a lot of reasons."

"Such as?"

"Such as carrying a baby for that long and then having to push it out of my body. Which is no joke considering our size difference," I point out, gesturing between us. "I've heard how difficult that labor was for the other women."

He nods. "I see."

"And also the fact that it's so damn dangerous here, and only getting more so. These invaders don't seem like they're going to stop coming any time soon. Not with the galactic fighting rings apparently raking in the money. How can we really keep children safe?" That's a hard truth about the future. "And...and what if I'm not a good mother?" I shake my head. "It isn't like I've had the best parenting examples. What if I mess our kid up?"

I hunch my shoulders, feeling that doubt. All of what I said was true. But that last bit strikes at the core of me.

"Fallon," Arawn murmurs, his arms coming around me from behind. I don't even know when he left the stool. "I think you are strong, intelligent, brave, and caring—you would make an excellent mother. However." He turns me around gently, raising his hands to cup my face. "It is not a requirement. I would love you if we never formed another generation. I am yours. And, I believe, in my heart...you are mine."

I stare up at him, at the painful sincerity in his eyes as I blink away the tears that have gathered in mine.

Not only has he not taken offense, he's saying everything I needed to hear but didn't even know to hope for. I don't know how to respond with words, my throat closing with emotion. So I don't use them.

Reaching up to slide my fingers into his hair, I tug Arawn down to me, laying a kiss on him. A kiss that says everything I'm feeling. Everything I want.

Arawn doesn't disappoint. Sliding his hands down my back, he grips my butt and lifts me up to make kissing me easier. His lips are soft and hungry under mine.

I missed this so much, missed this connection even as I ran away from it.

He doesn't wait to take me down to the soft pallet. He pulls at my clothes, just as I tug at his, both of our hands getting tangled as we try to continue touching the entire time. But neither of us stops.

Eventually, we're naked, skin against skin.

Arawn leaves my lips, kissing his way down my neck,

stopping and lingering on my breasts. I sigh as he kisses and licks every inch of them, his broad shoulders blocking out everything but him.

Then he moves lower. Pushing my legs apart, he settles my thighs on his shoulders, and then takes a moment just to look at me.

"Arawn..." I whisper, feeling my entire body blush at that intent look.

"You are so beautiful, Fallon," he says, looking up at me. "Perfect."

I don't know about that, but when his mouth is so close to the promised land, I'm not going to start arguing.

I bite back a moan as his hot mouth settles over me, his tongue sliding through my already wet folds.

I want him. Badly. But it feels like I always do. Even when I thought I didn't like him, I wanted him. And matters have only gotten worse the more time we spend together.

I arch up into his mouth, wanting to be even closer to the pleasure. I don't know how it's possible he never did this before me. It never felt awkward or clunky in any way. And he's a fast learner.

He doesn't mess around this time, his tongue finding my clit and working at it without surcease, the flick of his tongue divine. Closer...I feel the orgasm building, the tension winding tighter.

"Arawn!" I cry, as it hits me sooner than I expected.

I buck against his mouth, but he just holds me in place and licks me through it.

When I go limp, he flips me over to my stomach. Lifting one my legs up and out to the side, he layers himself over me and slowly slides inside.

I groan at the stretch, at the feeling of being utterly surrounded by his large body. I'm never going to get used to his size.

He moves my hair aside and kisses the back of my neck, my shoulders, every part of me he can reach as he starts to thrust slowly. I push back against him, loving the feeling of being so utterly full.

Of him.

"Fallon," he sighs, his face coming down to rest against the side of mine. He rubs it against mine, his breath hot as it fans over my cheek.

"Hmm."

It's slow and steady.

Until the very end.

Arawn pushes into me harder, sliding in even deeper.

And then he locks into place as his entire body shudders over mine, his cock pulsing inside me as he comes.

"My turn."

I push back, and he lets me topple him onto his back. I climb on top of him, taking in his flushed face and glittering eyes, his hair mussed. I reach down to grab his second cock. Never a thought I'd thought I'd have, but there you go. Arawn was nothing I ever expected to have in my life. Why would this part of him be any different?

Gripping the thick length in my hand, I run my thumb over the ridges along its length. I know they're the reason it feels that extra bit better when he's inside me. I bite my lip as I angle it up, adjusting the tip so it nudges into my entrance. Arawn's hands come up to grip my hips, his eyes scanning my body. And locking on where he is so close to going inside.

"Fallon, please," he groans, arching up and sliding in a half an inch.

I hum in response. That's exactly what I want too. So I don't make either of us wait any longer. I lower myself slowly, gasping as the angle hits another part of me inside.

Arawn grits his teeth, his fingertips digging into my hips when he's all the way in.

I take a moment, feeling like I'm full up to my throat. Wiggling to adjust, I pause as the ridge at the very base of him hits me...just...right. Leaning forward to brace my hands against his shoulders, I grind against him a little, closing my eyes. I could almost...a small orgasm hits me, making me clench my thighs around Arawn's hips.

With a growl, he flips us so I'm on the bottom again. And then he thrusts into me hard and fast, bracing my legs along his chest, a hand gripping each one. His eyes are shut tight, his jaw clenched as he thrusts. Like he needs it. Needs it right then.

That, coupled with the ridges hitting me with each thrust, push me over again. I cry out, my hands reaching out to grip Arawn's sides as I clench down on him. With a grunt of effort, he slings all the way in and follows me over, his body trembling above me. I take a deep breath as the orgasm slowly washes away once more.

Am I dead? What a way to go.

Arawn drops down next to me, pulling me into my side. Like he can't stand not to have as much contact as possible even after reconnecting.

"I want to mate you," he says abruptly.

"Huh?" I ask, opening my eyes, still enjoying the afterglow. "I think that might be what we just did," I remark, chuckling.

He turns my head towards his, so he can meet my eyes.

"No, Fallon," he says seriously. "I want an official mating. Including the ceremony. I want all of it."

"Oh." I stare at him, processing what he's saying. And then feeling the butterflies in my stomach, that warm rise of...happiness. "The people against the tradition will be really pissed at you."

He smiles, sliding my hair behind my ear.

"They will live. How do you feel? That is all that matters." He cups the side of my face. "Do you want to be my mate?"

I feel my lips curve into a smile of their own at the question. And then into a full-blown grin. I can't seem to control it at all. The burst of joy inside me is uncontainable.

"Yes," I say simply.

The flash of elation across his face warms me even more as he leans down and kisses me deeply.

Claiming me.

And I claim him right back.

"Good," he says, his lips brushing mine. "Then it is settled."

"I guess it is," I agree.

I snuggle into him when he lies back down, happy and drowsy. This is so much more than I expected. It's so much better. It takes me a while to fall asleep, the excitement of everything keeping me up in the best way possible. Eventually, I do drift off, feeling like everything in life is perfect.

I should know better than to think that now.

I should have been able to predict our wakeup call would be anything but.

"Arawn! Fallon! Wake up! We're being attacked!"

My eyes snap open at the voice, there and gone. It was one of the women, maybe Nora. But that doesn't matter.

Arawn is already on his feet, reaching for his clothes and his lochaber. I follow suit, slipping into my clothes before reaching for my weapon.

He's already out of the cave well before me, his long legs and quicker reflexes giving him a good edge. When I get outside, I see that the Zmaj are on the other side of the wall. When I slow down and peer around them, I see the group of those alien invaders rushing towards us once more.

The people on watch did their job well. I know the new guard positions were one of the things the Zmaj spoke about at the strategy meeting. Tidbits of what was discussed had floated around while we all ate.

"That's...a lot of them," Nora murmurs next to me.

I nod, feeling grim. It really is.

"Yeah. This is going to be—"

Before I can finish, a meteorite plummets through the air and hits the quickly narrowing space between the invaders and the Zmaj, sending sand spraying through the air.

Shit!

Again!?

"Meteorite shower!" I shout along with the others who saw it, to warn everyone still rushing out.

We turn and run just as the invaders are forced to retreat as well.

The Zmaj wait to make sure they do and then come back behind the wall and rush into the caves with us.

"Can you believe the meteorites fell again?" Nora whispers once we're under cover.

I shake my head. This is the second time it's happened when we were being attacked, stopping the impending battle. Only even earlier, before we could even begin the fight.

"Maybe Bashir is right," I quip. "Maybe Tajss is supernatural. Maybe it's protecting us."

At least, I try to joke about it, but it doesn't come off very funny.

Nora nods. "Maybe," she agrees seriously.

I feel a shiver of something. Maybe unease. What if the planet is...aware somehow?

Arawn reaches my side, sliding an arm around me and hugging me close. I lean against him for comfort, looking around at everyone. At the grim faces the Zmaj wear. The lingering traces of fear and shock among the women.

The atmosphere is heavy with the knowledge that the invaders aren't going anywhere. They're only growing more aggressive. With luck, the second shower in such a short period of time will convince them to leave for now. But we can't rely on meteor showers forever.

They've just bought us time to adjust and plan for what's coming.

EPILOGUE

ARAWN

I leave the city and travel out to the desert around it. I judge the distance carefully, stopping when I believe I have hit the estimate we agreed upon. Lifting the communication device to my mouth, I attempt to make contact.

"Do you hear me?"

I expect to wait a beat, but Addison's voice comes out crystal clear almost instantly.

"Yes! Yes, we do hear you! Woohoo!"

I grin as hear the commotion in the background as everyone begins to celebrate. Errol, Addison, and the rest of the team working on the technology aspect have been toiling tirelessly to integrate the meteorite glass. The comm-receiver is the first piece they've managed to successfully resurrect.

Now that we know it works outside the city limits, we can test it incrementally farther. The ability to communicate across distances...

It would improve the lives of nearly everyone on Tajss.

It would make the meetings we are currently embroiled

in between the Tribe, the city, and the mining settlement infinitely simpler if representatives did not have to physically be in the same area.

It could also be lifesaving if any one of the settlements requires aid in a timely manner. We cannot shorten the distances between the three points but having instantaneous communication would effectively cut the time it would take for aid to reach those in need in half.

"Come back, Arawn," Errol says, taking the comm device from Addison. "We will need to go in teams to travel out any farther."

"I am coming."

Currently, I am still in sight of the guards in charge of keeping a lookout, watchful for threats. But any farther would indeed be a risk, and Fallon would not be happy with me if I take it.

I am smiling as I travel back to the city, thinking of my beautiful mate.

When we announced our plans to have a mating cere-mony of our own, resistance was surprisingly difficult to find.

"They have bigger things to worry about right now," Fallon had commented, a twinkle in her eye. "They don't care about the mating ceremony anymore."

"Perhaps," I acknowledged. "It is a bad time to quibble over things that do not matter to anyone else really."

Since the multiple attacks we have already experienced, all of the settlements have prioritized meetings and working together. Even the New Village hasn't raised the fuss they usually do. They cannot deny that the human-and-Zmaj-populated territories need to be united if we have any chance of neutralizing the threat of the invaders.

That threat has settled over us like a sickness waiting to

strike. If we are to survive, we must work together. It is an undeniable reality.

Once in the city, I hurry towards the building the tech team is in, wanting to get back to Fallon. She is currently spending time with the other females she is close to. I was glad when she agreed to come with me to the city, glad she had people she likes to visit here. I feel too anxious leaving her behind with the Tribe after the attacks we have already faced there. I clench my jaw. It is a grim time indeed when I do not feel secure leaving my mate with the Tribe. But this is how it will be until we figure out a solution.

I reach the correct building and bound up the steps to the correct floor. The atmosphere is decidedly excited.

"Stay, we are going to celebrate," Errol urges, taking the device from me when I offer it.

I shake my head. "Fallon is likely waiting for me."

"Ah." He smiles. "I understand."

"Yeah, we do," Addison calls out, wagging her brows at me.

I shake my head, laughing as I leave the room. I do not mind the teasing. In fact, I enjoy it. Everyone thinks of Fallon and me as a unit now. Which is exactly as it should be.

I hurry back to the apartment we stay in while in the city, worrying if Fallon is back yet. I feel my chest fill with warmth when she opens the door to me.

"Hello," she greets me, smiling as she tugs me inside. "How did the test go?"

"Perfectly." I pull her into my arms and give her the kiss I've been thinking about giving her since I left.

"Hmm." She wraps her arms around my neck and kisses me back. When she breaks it, we are both breathing hard. "I love you, Arawn," she says huskily.

I feel my chest fill with that same all-encompassing emotion, so beautiful it almost hurts.

"I love you, Fallon," I murmur, cupping her face.

I trace her beloved features with my eyes. This is why I work so hard to contribute to the Tribe, to contribute to our settlements as I can. I need to keep Fallon safe. And to keep her safe...we all need to work together.

We all need to be strong.

And I will do everything in my power to ensure we are.

THE END

ABOUT THE AUTHOR

USA Today Bestselling Author of fantasy and scifi romance, Miranda Martin's books feature larger than life heroes with out-of-this-world anatomy and smart heroines destined to save the world. As a little girl she would sneak off with her nose in a book, dreaming of magical realms. Today she brings those fantasies to life and adores every fan who chooses to live in them for a while.

She was born and raised in southern Virginia, but as a veteran she's traveled to places like Korea, Hawaii and good 'ole Texas. Now she's settled in Kansas, the heart of America, with her husband and daughters. Her favorite animals are dragons, unicorns and cats. If she's not writing, you can still find her tucked away somewhere with a warm blanket and her nose in a book.

Get in touch!
mirandamartinromance.com
miranda@mirandamartinromance.com

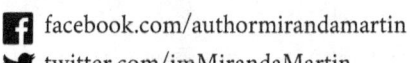

facebook.com/authormirandamartin
twitter.com/imMirandaMartin
instagram.com/imMirandaMartin